D1647975

JUN 0 7 2004

Unveiling

Unveiling

A NOVEL

Suzanne M. Wolfe

PARACLETE PRESS
BREWSTER, MASSACHUSETTS

Library of Congress Cataloging–in–Publication Data

Wolfe, Suzanne M.
    Unveiling : a novel / Suzanne M. Wolfe.
        p.   cm.
    ISBN 1–55725–354–4
        1. Painting, Medieval—Conservation and restoration—
Fiction. 2. Americans—Italy—Fiction. 3. Divorced women—
Fiction. 4. Art restorers—Fiction 5. Rome (Italy)—Fiction. I.
Title.
    PS3573.O5266U585 2004
    813' .54—dc22
                                                2003026114

10 9 8 7 6 5 4 3 2 1

Published by Paraclete Press
Brewster, Massachusetts
www.paracletepress.com
Printed in the United States of America.

For my mother

" Every act of cleaning
is an act of critical interpretation."
CESARE BRANDI

Acknowledgments

For their patience and support over the years, I'm grateful to a host of friends and colleagues.

Harold Fickett was the first to recognize a glimmer of potential in my early attempts to write fiction. He also served as my unofficial agent for a time.

During my years at the Milton Center in Wichita, Kansas, I was enriched by the fellowship of writers at the Friday Workshop.

A.G. Harmon's critiques of the initial drafts were enormously helpful. His novel, *A House All Stilled* (University of Tennessee Press), taught me more about writing than he will ever know.

Writer and editor Phyllis Tickle read the first draft of this novel. Later, a word from her helped this book find its publisher.

My agent, Carol Mann, has been a steadfast supporter for over a decade now.

My colleagues in the English department at Seattle Pacific University have provided a stimulating environment in which to work. Special thanks to Luke Reinsma, who read the novel in draft form.

Lil Copan, my editor and friend, has one of the best ears for literary fiction I have ever encountered. Thanks for not letting me get away with anything!

My children, Magdalen, Helena, Charles, and Benedict, learned—eventually—that Mom needed some space to do this thing. Thanks, guys.

Finally, thanks to my husband Greg, for his heroic support over the years, especially his willingness to take our children on a month-long odyssey in the Southwest this past summer so I could complete the novel.

Side Panel
ONE

I

DROPLETS OF RAIN SKITTERED DOWN THE BARS as Rachel pushed open the wrought iron gate. Entering a small courtyard, she climbed a peeling, ochre-washed staircase that led to the second floor. Above her head a series of clotheslines divided the sky into pieces of a puzzle.

Heels scraping against stone, shoulders burning from the deadweight of her bags, Rachel willed herself up the last few steps to her *pensione*. On either side of her door, withered tendrils trailed out of two large concrete urns of vaguely neoclassical design, tangling in overgrown chaos over the walkway.

As she fitted the key into the lock, her cell phone rang.

"Rachel, is that you?"

Rachel chinned the phone to her shoulder and edged through the door with her luggage.

"I've been trying to get a hold of you."

"Sorry."

"When did you get in?"

"Couple of hours ago. Had to go straight to the museum." In Rome to direct the conservation of a panel painting in one of the churches, the project was being coordinated by Rome's Ferrara Museum and promised to take anywhere from three to six months.

She dropped her bags and toed the door shut behind her. Her coat sleeve got jammed in a crisscross of straps as she tried to shrug her computer and purse off her shoulder onto the bed. She swore, transferring the cell phone to her hand as she shed the heavy wool, then sat down, rubbing wearily at her eyes, at her face. The skin felt taut, transparent. Holding the phone loosely in her palm, the voice suddenly became thin, tinny, taut as strung wire.

Hooke's Law.

It was the only thing Rachel remembered from physics class at school: that if a spring is stretched too far by an inordinate weight it can never return to its original tension. The scribbled formulae on the blackboard had been gibberish, but she hadn't forgotten the name, nor the sensation of sinews thinning to breaking point.

She brought the phone closer.

" . . . divorce . . . running off to Rome—"

"Look," Rachel said. "Gotta go. I'll e-mail."

Her words collided with a snatch of Italian beneath the crackle as if the lines had gotten crossed and the sound bounced back. Then a click.

Rachel hit the off button and tossed the phone onto the bed. The *proprietaria* had drawn back the covers to reveal an inseam of cream lace running the width of the turned down sheet, the cotton releasing a sun-bleached, wind-flapped scent. A heavy brass bedstead rose above the stacked pillows at the head, the metal streaked and dulled by age.

Squat, paint-chipped radiators set against the walls pumped out a thick felty heat that made the three-barred electric fire opposite the bed look superfluous. French doors opened out onto a balcony that overhung the street. Nothing like as big as her Manhattan apartment, but located at the heart of Rome, and, above all, anonymous. No inquisitive neighbors, no unexpected calls from well-meaning friends.

The clang of a single bell calling the faithful to vespers, the sound carrying true and clear in the winter air, drew Rachel to the balcony, her breath pluming white in the dank air. Beneath the balcony, a narrow, cobbled street sloped towards a main road to the left and the river Tiber beyond. It was growing dark and a cold wind was picking up from the north, tumbling the litter in the street. In the distance, she could make out the dome of a basilica rounding against a greenish sky, and Rachel suddenly felt dispirited. Maybe her mother was right, maybe taking this job in Rome was nothing more than an inability to face up to the failure of her marriage, her life.

Despite filing for divorce, feeling a winded sense of relief when she saw Mark's signature at the bottom of the settlement papers, she felt oddly disconnected now that she had removed herself from the familiar framework of her life. Over lunch with a girlfriend the week before, her trip had sounded sensible, even brave.

"I'd be a basketcase," her friend said. "*Was* a basket-case. Will be again." She raised her glass and gave Rachel a toast. "Here's to alimony." Her friend was already on her second failing marriage.

But to be honest, Rachel felt the same disconnect in New York. Up at seven, at the museum by nine, home by seven. On a good day time spooled by; she would look up from a section of canvas and realize that she had lost three hours. Meetings, phone calls, e-mails kept her conscious mind skimming, while beneath the surface her true self felt as if it were moving in water. But no matter how rapidly the hours passed while she worked on her paintings, Rachel felt her body tense when she reentered her apartment each evening. She wanted to draw time out, to trick it into standing still. She lingered longer and longer in the shower, tried on endless combinations of clothes, anything to delay the moment when she would look around her and realize that her belongings, her life, her face in the mirror, were alien. She would wander from kitchen to living room, picking up this book, putting it down, picking up another. An unwashed glass in the sink would bother her until she rinsed it and set it on the rack. Then she would return ten minutes later to dry it and put it away. Like living in zero gravity, everything solid in her life had come adrift and if she didn't pin them down they would float away.

Her friends told her this was normal, a type of post-divorce stress, but Rachel knew better. A ghost in her life long before Mark, she thought marrying him would make her substantial again, give her heft in a universe that came to her more and more like bad TV reception, images moving beneath pixels of snow. Only the paintings she restored were real, things she could see and touch and know that they were fixed, faithful. Now even that was threatened, along with the museum in Manhattan where she worked.

Originally built in the shape of a castle, the massive brownstone had been the home of a shipping magnate in the nineteenth century. It was an oddity amidst the chrome and glass of midtown and looked more like a hotel than a museum. Now the twenty-first century had caught up with it, and a vast structure of metal and glass erupted out of the left side of the east wing, bone splintering from a wound. Every day for the past year she watched the hole grow larger as the steel worked its way out, and she had felt sickened and helpless.

She remembered how the museum shuddered when they broke through the walls and how the shock of it passed into her body and remained there, reverberating long after the silence settled. Later, a mist of powdered stone began to sift through the air like fine sugar until she could write her name on practically any surface in the museum. White and gritty and pervasive as memory, she could taste it on her tongue.

Mark, her ex, was the architect who designed the new wing. There had even been a feature on him in *New York* magazine four months ago. He came into her office and tossed it onto her desk, and in that article she learned that her altarpiece—the one she labored for two years to restore—was to be housed there permanently. Hidden from the Nazis during World War II, it was discovered moldering in the crypt of a Bavarian church and sent to Rachel's museum for extensive restoration and reconstruction. Now it was to exchange the verdant horizons that inspired its minute background landscapes for a blank room ceilinged with halogen tubing and humming with dehumidifiers, temperature gauges and a sophisticated fire-alarm system. Instead of being visited by a congregation of believers, of people who could trace their lineage back to the time when the altarpiece was painted, perhaps even claim kinship to the artist himself, it was to become an altarpiece without an altar, an anachronism as out of place as the museum itself.

She looked up from the article to find Mark studying her, his eyes blank, the ghost of a smile creasing the edges of his mouth. The whine of a drill and the voices of workmen calling to each other punctuated the silence between them. There were no children so she supposed putting her altarpiece in the new wing was the same as getting custody.

After he left she picked up the phone and punched an extension. She would take the curator up on his offer to send her to Rome. The Apex Corporation, an American conglomerate eager to make a name for itself as a patron of the arts, was sponsoring a restoration project in conjunction with her own museum.

The light grew dimmer, the outline of the buildings increasingly indistinct as dusk rapidly accelerated towards night. A lamp clicked on in a window opposite and Rachel thought she saw a hand lift in greeting. She stepped back inside and latched the shutters. Going into the bathroom, she turned the bathwater on full until steam began to fog the mirror over the sink.

At least she had made it to the meeting on time. At one point she thought her flight would be rerouted through Heathrow, London, and she would be forced to change planes. A winter storm barreling down the coast out of Canada had backed up planes all along the Eastern seaboard transforming La Guardia into a seething irritable mass. She'd landed at Leonardo da Vinci four hours ago, taken the commuter train into the center of Rome, then a taxi straight to the museum.

A woman showed her into the library of the Ferrera Museum and asked her to wait. A series of tall bookcases lined the walls, three to each side and two at either end. She ran her fingertips along the spine of a volume feeling for the bite of the gold-embossed lettering in the velvet of the calfskin. Tier upon tier of shelves rose to a series of semi-circular lunettes depicting scenes from classical mythology, then on to the vaulted ceiling where a monumental white hand wandered over the head of a sleeping adolescent lolling between a woman's heavy breasts, his legs straddling her hips. It was at once gorgeous and utterly indecent. A secular Pieta with a powerful sexual kick.

Above the youth's curls Rachel saw a face of exquisite blankness, as inhumanly archetypal as that of a primitive fertility goddess. Venus's lips curled upwards in the sly smile of sexual possession as she looked down on Rachel through slitted eyes.

"Dr. Piers, I see our painting interests you."

A man came towards her from the opposite end of the room, the sound of his shoes tapping smartly on the marble floor unnaturally amplified by the large room.

"Rubens," she said. "Early."

"A bit, how you say, flamboyant, no? The passion of youth," the man smiled. "This house was owned by Cardinal Ferrera in the seventeenth century. But allow me to introduce myself. I am Dr. Persegati." His handshake was firm, brief, and businesslike. "Welcome to Rome." With graying hair combed straight back from his forehead and glistening with an oil that gave off a faint scent of cloves, he spoke with a deliberate precision that would have sounded phony in unaccented tones.

"Forgive me. I know you must be exhausted, but I want to introduce you to the others. Please to follow me." Walking to a door on the far side of the room, he opened it, sweeping his left arm wide to indicate that Rachel should precede him. "I have followed your work on the Baultenheimer Altarpiece with the greatest of interest. Your paper was very fine, especially the pigment sample analysis. As you argued, the piece must surely have originated in a monastic community in the Ruhr Valley. *Brava!*"

A yellowing pockmarked mirror set in a gilt frame flashed her image at her as she followed him down a corridor, undulating over the irregular surface, distorting weirdly. Pale skin surrounded by dark swatches of hair, gray eyes.

Persegati opened a door. A fireplace in black marble bespoke a halfhearted attempt at grandiosity, but the effect was somber, even depressing. Perhaps this was where the cardinal had transacted business. No Venus.

A man stood by the window, his back to her. Next to him, a young woman who looked like a student. As if they had just shared a joke, a faint sense of camaraderie hung in the air.

"May I introduce Dr. Piers from the Eliot-Simpson Museum in Manhattan."

The air in the room cranked from loose to tight.

"Honored to meet with you, Dr. Piers," the girl said. Her dark hair was cut in a symmetrical bob, and when she moved the razored tips swung along her jaw and touched the corners of her mouth. "My name is Pia Amata."

"Rachel."

"Pia will intern as your research assistant," said Persegati. "Her involvement constitutes the *practica* part of her doctorate on late medieval manuscripts."

Rachel turned to the man by the window.

"Nigel Thompson." His fingers, cool and supple, clasped hers briefly.

"Dr. Thompson is on sabbatical from the National Gallery in London," Persegati explained. "He is chief curator of their medieval collection."

He had the prematurely stooping carriage of an Oxford don but the deep crosshatching at the corners of his eyes gave him a shrewd look. An expert in his field, he was a world authority on panel painting and the restoration of frames. Only his sabbatical status precluded him from being the primary in this project.

"I'm your lab man. Currently working on a fifteenth century Umbrian panel. Shocking condition. Fractured in several places and the surface legibility's severely impaired by abrasion and paint loss. Donati's giving me a hand with it."

"Where is he?" Rachel said. "I was told he'd be here." She was pleased when she learned she was going to be working with him. Part of an international team that recently identified some lost Van Eyck miniatures, his pigment analysis had been key.

"He'll take you to the site tomorrow," Pia said, glancing at Nigel.

Rachel saw the look and wondered at it. She took out her diary and turning to a blank page in the back, wrote quickly. "If it's OK with everyone, we'll meet again here tomorrow at noon." She tore out the page, ripped it in half, and handed one each to Pia and Nigel. "In the meantime, if you have any questions, this is my cell phone number and the address where I'm staying."

While the bath was filling, she undressed, bare feet hopping and shrinking from the chill of the floor tiles. Lowering herself, she slid along the bottom until she could stretch out and lay her head back against the ledge.

Second-guessing herself for coming to Rome was pointless. The new project would perform its usual magic, take her to a place where Mark, her mother, the mess she had made of her life would drop away, become irrelevant. Her ability to lose herself in her work was one of Mark's complaints during their marriage.

Rachel hooked a strand of hair over her ear.

Sometime during the second year of marriage her "zen focus," as he called it when they first met, changed to an accusation of aloofness, usually when she didn't want to go to some dinner party or gallery opening. Marooned in a sea of chatter, the feeling she sometimes got at the zoo when she was a child would return, as if subject and object had switched places. She wondered what the paintings made of the diamonds, the Rolexes and the acres of very chic, very PC, faux fur stoles. Materializing out of the passionate torque of oil and tempera, the gallery walls were peopled with figures from another century, another culture, the creation of fevered brushstrokes that went unheeded, unseen, while the business of art in the twenty-first century continued unabated.

Disgust with that world, Mark's world, had driven her to Rome. And deeper still, just beneath the surface, something else. Depression, some called it; *acedia* was the medieval word. Rachel knew it as soulsickness—an old, familiar acquaintance.

She shifted her hips. Sloshing and knocking against her skin, the water subsided gradually into stillness until all she could hear was the hollow plunk of the faucet dripping every now and then into the water by her toes.

Peaceful. Predictable.

II

HAIR SPILLING INTO HER EYES, Rachel sat up completely disoriented. Pale, lemony light filtered through the open door.

"*Scusa.*"

She saw a figure in the doorway. A woman holding a mop and bucket, a loose cardigan hanging from bony shoulders. Her landlady. The creak of the door must have woken her.

"I come back."

"No, no, wait. What time is it?"

"Ten."

She'd overslept. Swinging her legs over the edge of the bed, she reached for her robe.

"A *signore* come by an hour ago. He left you this." The woman held out a scrap of paper.

"*Grazie.*" Ink bled into spidery veins making the writing difficult to read, the edges furled with damp. *Meet you at the church — Donati.*

A man was sitting on the steps of Our Lady of Sorrows at the far end of the piazza. Behind him an order of Corinthian columns fluted upwards in an elegant, austere semi-circle. Disappearing beneath the half-porch, a massive, double door filigreed with ironwork and star-shaped studs. The man was smoking, thin spirals twisting over his head, momentarily blue as they hung in the air, then shredding to gray as the breeze caught and lifted them. The material of his coat pulled taut as he rested his arms on his knees, wrinkling in shooting lines at the shoulder when he lifted the cigarette to his lips. Seeing her, he stood up, his movements fluid, composed. Eyes assessing, veiled, Rachel felt him studying her as he approached. Hair that appeared black in the shadows revealed itself to be brown when the light hit it.

"I trust you didn't have any trouble finding the church," he said.

"None at all."

"*Bene.*" He flicked away his cigarette. "This way."

Instead of ascending the steps under the colonnaded portico, Donati led her around the side of the church to a small, low-linteled door. It had no handle, just a gaping keyhole and an iron grille set below eye-level in the center. Donati thudded on it with the heel of his hand, the blows echoing somewhere within.

Footsteps approached. The panel behind the grille cracked open a finger's width.

"*Vattene!*" a voice said.

"*Sono Giovanni.*"

A pause, a nub of metal in the keyhole, then a wedge of darkness widening as the door opened.

They found themselves at the top of a flight of steps with a passageway leading off to their right.

15

"This is Angelo," Donati said. "He looks after the church."

"*Ciao.*" Rachel's hand closed around fingers that fluttered restlessly, then were snatched back.

As her eyes adjusted to the light she saw that Angelo was short, his head reaching only to Donati's elbow. He wore a long tunic that blended with the shadows like natural camouflage. Disproportionately small features floated, unmoored, in a vast expanse of white flesh. It gave him an incomplete look as if he had been born before they had knitted together properly. A broad forehead rose sheer to a thinning hairline. Currant eyes behind thick lenses squinted at her myopically. She realized Angelo had Downs Syndrome.

Donati said something in Italian that Rachel didn't catch. Angelo nodded and pattered ahead down the steps.

Columns soared in symmetrical rows, trunks of an ancient forest, petrified and monumental, bearing the weight of the entire church. The crypt was cold, and except for the sound of their footsteps, silent. Stone faces, some angelic, others impish, thrust at them from the carved corners of the capitals. Flush with the floor, a gravestone with a name and date on it, so worn as to be almost unreadable.

Crossing the crypt, they came to another flight of steps which emerged behind the altar at the apex of the nave. Stained glass flung jewels of color at Rachel's feet—red, blue and brilliant green. A chased, silver cross glowed on the altar. The copper chains of the sanctuary lamp stirred in the faint draught from the crypt, links clashing softly. Compared to the desolation of the crypt with its brooding emptiness, the sanctuary, though

16

sparse, seemed lived in, used. Rachel felt as if she had inadvertently opened the door of a bedroom in a strange house. Noiselessly, almost guiltily, she opened the low gate that divided the *sanctum* from the church and slipped through, alone.

Banks of candles in tiered stands stretched along the northern aisle. Above, on stone cornices jutting from each column, stood the saints, some of painted wood, others carved from stone, their identities so effaced that all that remained was a hand raised in blessing, the sway of a robed hip that had once carried the Christchild. Here and there a petitionary note curled out from beneath the plinth of a statue.

Beneath the groined arches were a series of side chapels, interspersed with wooden confessionals with dusty velvet curtains and cracked leather kneelers. Rachel saw votive candles burning on an altar. She entered a small chapel. Prie dieux grouped haphazardly gave it a workaday look, as if frequently used. A missal lay open on a kneeler, a yellow tassel marking a page.

Quarried from a single block of stone, the surface of the altar was deeply pitted but free of cracks. The votives, round, flat candles in shallow copper bowls, were arranged in a semi-circle. Behind them, bolted securely to the wall and stretching the full length of the altar, Rachel saw the panels of a large triptych.

The frame, bored with tiny holes, gold leaf dulled and densely crackled through drying, appeared largely intact. No missing pieces and only a couple mechanical cracks—wide fissures caused by rough handling or accidents, like being dropped—in the wood itself. Infra-red scans would tell her if there was evidence of cradling, a well-meaning but misguided attempt at preventing warping in an earlier conservation era.

An unmistakable massing of figures dominated the foreground of the central panel. Rachel counted three heads; two side by side, roughly on a level with each other, the third lower down and tilted at an unnatural angle. Here and there spots of color came through—indigo, aquamarine, vermilion—but in such somber tones she couldn't be sure if they were the result of deterioration of the original pigments or caused by the tonal deadening of varnish. Behind them, perfectly centered, rose a vertical bar that seemed to disappear out of the picture at the top. No horizontal line bisected it. If that were the cross, then it was an unusual rendering. More commonly, it might be a tree with the lower branches obscured. If so, then she was probably looking at the *Flight into Egypt.*

"What do you think?" Donati was leaning against the gate to the chapel. Rachel wondered how long he had been standing there.

"No evidence of cracking or worm holes on the panels themselves. That's good news. My guess is the soot and tallow from the candles have formed a protective coating, although it could be a later application of varnish." Gluey, resin varnish, dulled original colors to a uniform umber, toning down blues, whites and greens, lightening darker colors, effectively destroying the entire tonal range of the piece. Removing the varnish was the only way to come at the original pigments.

"I need to know the exact layers I'm dealing with, working from the base up."

Donati nodded. "Type of wood; how many coats of gesso; whether there's a layer of *bole* as a ground for any gold leaf; the paint and its exact oil content; last of all, varnish. I'll take a cross-section from the edge." He opened his backpack, took out a small case of test tubes and began to scrape minute fragments of varnish from the triptych. "In the meantime this will tell us what's on the surface."

"And type of solvent we use."

"Acetone?"

"To take off the varnish, if there is any, but once we get down to the paint it'll be too harsh. Don't want to blanch the paint underneath, or God forbid, remove it altogether. That's key. Chemical analysis should tell us if the original paint is susceptible to solvent." Some artists used natural waxes and resins that dissolved in solvent, a restorer's worst nightmare, especially if the artist had experimented with impermanent and unstable pigments.

Solvent would have to be applied delicately, on the end of a Q-Tip, circling over one tiny space at a time, perhaps varying in strength depending on the painter's technique in applying his paint. A finicky task. Rarely did an artist employ a uniform technique over the entire panel or canvas.

"White spirit, then."

"Mmm." The interplay of angles and lines belied the theme of rest in the *Flight*. Dragging downward, the dense concentration of shadow at the base acted like a powerful gravitational pull. She pointed to the side panels. "Look at this." The faint hint of a background, perhaps the outline of a building. Undulating lines suggested hills.

"Geographical location?" Donati indicated the lower sections closest to the candles. "Saints or donors. No way of knowing."

"No," Rachel agreed. "But let's get infra-red scans set up. I need to know if there's any preliminary modeling under the paint, and, if so, whether it differs from the figures painted over them. If the triptych's ever been retouched, we'll know the extent and the time period."

"*Pentimenti*," said Donati.

"Yes." Repentances. Oddly sinister word for artistic alterations. "We need to x-ray the frame. Maybe the damage is just superficial. Once we know the extent, we'll be able to dismantle the whole thing and shift it to the lab."

Donati looked at the panels again. "Can I make a suggestion?"

"Fire away."

"Restore the triptych on site."

Rachel thought for a moment. "The integrity of the panels could be threatened," she said. "I don't have enough information to make that call." Months of work for nothing if the frame disintegrated. Donati must know that.

"Apart from those two cracks, there's no major structural damage. No cradling either. The frame's essentially sound."

"How do you know?"

"I've done a preliminary examination."

Rachel's fingers fumbled one of the straps on her satchel. "On whose say-so?"

He shrugged. "Mine."

"Does Persegati know?"

"No."

"What about the others?"

"Only Nigel. He says he can deal with the frame later." He stoppered one of the tubes and labeled it.

"I know it's hard to conceive of it in its current condition, but this isn't just a work of art, it's a shrine of sorts."

Rachel thought of the notes tacked to the statues. The idea of suppliants muttering to the triptych filled her with distaste, a kind of dread. She would be forced to witness things that should be kept private, even secret. She also knew restoration was done on site all over Rome, inevitable in a city filled with priceless artifacts in a continual state of decay.

"I'd like to see the results of your tests," she said, "before I make a decision."

They worked in silence for two hours, Rachel measuring, jotting down a list of equipment necessary for the project, Donati collecting samples. The glass tubes clashed as he zipped up his case. "All set."

"I'll set up a raking light tomorrow," Rachel said. A relatively simple and non-invasive method to see if there was any damage or undermodeling. "Pia can start with the church records, find out when the triptych was acquired, and from whom. Start building up a history." She glanced at a bloom of damp on the wall to the left of the triptych. "Judging from the state of the church, I'd be surprised if they kept pristine records. But it's worth a try. Who knows, she may turn up the approximate time frame of a donation or commission."

They left the chapel, turning right towards the main entrance. It was noon. Mass had begun while they had been in the chapel. The priest was standing, arms stretched above his head, hands forming the cusp of a pyramid; the people were kneeling. A sudden pocket of silence, purple robes pouring down, a sliver of white held aloft. For a brief moment, enfolded within the timelessness of that one gesture, a gesture enacted over millennia and ratified with the blood of martyrs, Rachel glimpsed why Donati wanted the triptych to remain here. Brooding and somber, the painting belonged more to the half-light and murmuring than the pitiless scrutiny of science. Then a bell rang. The priest's arms fell, the people rose in one rustling motion.

Rachel saw Donati genuflect and make a rapid sign of the cross. Suddenly uncomfortable, she turned and left the church.

III

In the middle of the piazza, a circular basin, barely bigger than a baptismal font, rested on a worn pedestal, a naked cherub bending double under the bell-shaped pitcher hoisted over his shoulder at its center. Water snaked over the lip of the vessel in a thin line and plashed into the pool. Rachel walked over and let the ribbon play over her fingers, the water icy but clear. A plastic cup lay overturned on the basin's rim, rolling gently from side to side. She set it upright and looked about her.

Tall buildings constructed from blocks of ochre-colored stone framed the square on three sides. Round-topped windows, set at regular intervals, looked directly onto the piazza, weathered shutters thrown back. Opposite, an espresso bar and grocery store occupied the ground floor of one of the buildings. Stacked bistro chairs under the awning of the coffee shop awaited more clement temperatures. Bread baked in the shape of letters spelled out the grocery store's name, a sign in the window advertised neighborhood staples—*pane, sigeretta, lotteria*.

Mopeds lined one side of the piazza, oddly symmetrical and neat compared to the square's pervasive air of neglect. Pigeons fought for scraps from an overflowing dumpster.

Donati joined her at the fountain. "A bit run-down," he said, following the direction of her gaze. "Most of the young have abandoned the old neighborhoods."

"Same in New York." A newspaper flapped against Rachel's ankles as they began to walk.

"You live in Manhattan?" Donati asked.

"Upper West Side."

"You were there on 9/11?"

Rachel nodded. She'd been working on a canvas in the basement of her museum and felt rather than heard the deep boom as the first tower collapsed. A technician ran in, white-faced, and it was then that she learned about the attack. Outside the air was thick with smoke and the choking smell of charred meat. Sirens sounded continuously, hysterically, people were running, some standing frozen in the middle of traffic, looking up. An Orthodox Jew with black fedora and curly sidelocks was rocking back and forth, hands outstretched as if to receive the ashes falling from the sky. His lips were moving but only a thin wail emerged. That's how she had felt for months afterwards, as if all words had vaporized in the conflagration, leaving only a high keening, primitive, collective, inconsolable.

Like thousands of others she had made her pilgrimage to the site and looked down into the crater, the enormous grave of those whose pictures adorned every wall and telegraph pole in the city. Rachel was grateful Donati didn't press her for details. The memory of those faces, men and women, young and old, most smiling, some intense, all vibrantly alive, haunted her more powerfully than their obscene memorial of shattered stone and scorched earth.

They emerged into the Piazza Navona. A phone in a chrome booth near the fountain was ringing, repetitive, insistent, and oddly plaintive in that wide space. A newspaper vendor next to the booth ignored it as if he knew the call wasn't for him. The sound reminded her of the bell in the church and Donati's rapid gesture, forehead to breastbone, left to right, hand curving to favor the index finger. The movement possessed the fluidity of a habit learned in childhood, the hand's journey completed instinctively. He had been embarrassed when he noticed her looking at him as if he had inadvertently slipped into an accent that betrayed his origin.

The fountain was dry and filled with debris, the white marble figures mottled with algae. The obelisk in the center pointed to a muted sky.

They skirted the railings surrounding the fountain, walking past the steps of the church of St. Agnes.

Instead of taking the street leading to the Via Monterone, Donati made for one of the trattorias fronting the piazza. *Ubertino's*—the sign flashed with maddening regularity.

"I told the others we'd meet at the museum at noon," she said.

"Change of plan," Donati said. "Nigel thought it would be a good idea to meet over lunch."

The phone cut off as the door swung shut behind them.

Packed and stiflingly close after the raw emptiness of the piazza, the air thick with the smell of garlic and oil, the noise tremendous, the restaurant hummed with the midday rush. A man leaned over the countertop of the bar at the far end, a newspaper propped against an ashtray, a shot glass of amber liquid at his elbow which he sipped without raising his eyes from the print.

Donati exchanged greetings with the proprietor who ushered them to a table set for four. "Can I ask you something?" he said as Rachel draped her jacket on the back of her chair.

"Sure."

"Why is a mega corporation like Apex interested in an obscure little triptych in a Roman church? What's the angle?"

"No angle." Rachel shook out her napkin and spread it across her lap. "And if you're asking if I represent Apex, the answer's no. All I care about is the project. Apex is footing the bill. Simple."

"So what's the connection between your museum and Persegati?"

"His role is to smooth the way with Rome's conservation department."

"That all?"

"You don't like him, do you?"

Donati was saved from answering by Nigel and Pia's arrival. Pia leaned across the table and kissed Donati on both cheeks. "*Ciao.*"

Nigel nodded to Rachel.

"What do you think of the church?" Pia asked, sitting down next to her.

26

"Beautiful," Rachel said. The seventeenth century facade was Cortona's work, she knew. "But the inside seems much older than the facade. More gothic than baroque. Know anything about it?"

"The renovation was financed by the wealthiest banker of the era, Agostino Chigi," said Pia. "But unfortunately—or fortunately, if you prefer the medieval to the baroque—Chigi went bankrupt. The interior of the church was never even attempted, let alone finished."

The cruciform shape of the nave and transepts. Classic gothic.

"Like most churches here, there used to be a Roman temple on the site," Nigel said, taking up the account, "but the existing structure dates from the fourteenth century. It's said to have been the church of the *acquarelli,* the "water-sellers," who brought water from the nearby Tiber to parts of the city cut off from a fresh water supply."

The fountain in front of the church and the ancient altar in the chapel, possibly brought up from one of the catacombs on the outskirts of the city after Constantine permitted Christian worship within the city limits.

A waiter appeared. Rachel opened the menu but the profusion of entrees and courses killed her appetite. She ordered soup.

"Did you see the statue of the Virgin?" Nigel asked.

Rachel thought of the statues with the missing children in their arms. "Not sure. I may have."

"It's in one of the other side chapels."

"Then, no. I only went into the one containing the triptych."

"Legend has it that during the riots that followed the assassination of Giuliano de' Medici in the Pazzi conspiracy in the fifteenth century, the statue was struck by a stone and began to bleed."

Nigel filled her glass from a carafe of house red. "Superstition, of course. Anyway, this 'miracle' was taken by the people to be a divine condemnation of the current unrest and was quickly turned to full political advantage by Pope Sixtus IV. Soon after, the pope engineered a peace treaty and chose the church of Our Lady of Sorrows in which to give his celebratory mass. He renamed it the church of Mary of Divine Peace, but that didn't wash with the locals and they continued to call it by its original name."

She waited while the waiter ground black pepper over her bowl, dusting the air with fragrance. "OK," she said, picking up her spoon. "Let's begin. Pia, would you check the church records for a donation? Under both names. If we can find out when the triptych was acquired, or commissioned, we'll have something definite to cross-check with a carbon 14 dating." She looked at Donati. "I want you to go ahead with the pigment analysis followed by a carbon 14 dating. The pigment analysis I'll need right away so we can get started. Nigel, I assume you can help with that?"

"No problem."

"Once we know the chemical makeup of the pigments and how many layers of varnish we may have to remove, I want you to do an infra-red scan to see if there have been any touch-ups of the original. That'll keep you busy for a while. Meanwhile, I'll set up a raking light on site and see if I pick up any warping or splitting in the panels."

"My guess," Donati said, "is that this'll be more of a conservation job than strictly restoration. Judging from the intact condition of the frame, the panels are going to be in pretty good shape."

"Only if the panels are made from the same wood," Rachel said.

"Granted, but we detected no evidence of paint cracking or blistering."

"So far," Rachel said. "But God only knows what we'll find once we get rid of the varnish. If the paint starts to flake then we've got problems. We'll have to reattach it with heated spatulas."

"Bloody nuisance," Nigel said, fastidiously moving olives to the side of his plate. "I've spent the last six months doing nothing but."

"Let's hope it doesn't come to that," Rachel said. "I'd like to interfere with the integrity of the panels as little as possible. Anyone got a problem with that?" She glanced around the table. There were various schools of thought when it came to conservation. Some of the Louvre's projects, admittedly from a previous era, horrified her, paintings that ended up as glistening and pristine as the day they came off the artist's easel. The Cesare Brandi school that believed the work should be cleaned and stabilized for the long-term rather than refurbished using modern pigments, was the one she favored. Her job in overseeing the project was to ensure the delicate balance between the work's authenticity and its artistic legibility was preserved.

"Absolutely," Nigel said. "Interfere as little as possible." The others nodded.

"Good. Then the immediate question is whether we waste valuable time wrapping the frame in linen so we can move it, or whether we just go ahead and restore it in the church." She looked at Donati. "I need to see the results of your private tests," she said.

"I'll drop them by later."

The waiter came to clear their plates. Rachel handed him her American Express card. "Apex's tab," she said when Nigel protested. "One of the perks of mega-corporations," she added, glancing at Donati.

As they got up to leave, the man at the bar was draining his glass, the sports section folded under his arm, the rest of the newspaper discarded on the counter. It was almost three.

"Later," Donati said to Rachel. "*Ciao*, Nigel." He and Pia set off across the square, heads close. Rachel wondered if they were lovers.

"Don't mind him." Nigel fell in step beside her. "Trouble is his politics don't sit too well with the pragmatics of conservation."

"Politics?"

"Socialism."

"And Apex is the epitome of American capitalism."

"Exactly."

"I didn't notice him offering to pay for lunch."

Nigel laughed.

"Do you feel that way? About Apex, I mean," Rachel said.

"Good Lord, no. We both know that America practically floats Europe. Britain, for example, would be finished without American dollars. Cambridge, my alma mater, would sink into the fens without summer schools catering to Americans. No, no," he said, "I'm not impolite enough to bite the hand that feeds me. I leave that to idealists like Donati." They had stopped at an intersection, waiting for the light to change. "Listen," he said, suddenly serious. "Don't worry about him. He's good at what he does, the rest ignore. Pia is a gem, though." He bowed with ironic formality. "I bid you goodnight, Dr. Piers. Welcome to the Eternal City."

"Good night."

IV

RACHEL CROSSED THE ROAD, taking a side street towards her *pensione*. She walked briskly, keeping close to the buildings. At dusk traffic was picking up along the main thoroughfares although the smaller roads were still relatively empty. A moped rushed by, handlebars brushing her sleeve, exhaust hot against her legs. With its curves and meanders, its dead-end alleys, the leisurely pace of pedestrians in contrast to the swerve and swoosh of traffic and the unabashed eye contact of strangers, the city was more intimate than New York, and for that reason more dangerous.

The painting of a Madonna set behind glass and illuminated by a lamp regarded her from the side of a building as she rounded a corner and ducked through an archway. Rows of stalls were set up, people thronging about, fingering goods, haggling, everyone eager to finish shopping before the market closed. Boys carrying boxes dodged in and out of the crush, delivering groceries for customers, running errands for the shopkeepers. One ran past her. He had curly brown hair and large liquid eyes. "*Mi scusi!*" he panted as his box grazed her hip.

A smell of vegetation and fish hung in the air and beneath it the aroma of freshly ground coffee. She shouldered her way through the press, stopped to make a purchase, then passed a poultry vendor. A man with a blood-spattered apron and a white paper hat tilted over one eye stood at a wooden chopping board methodically cutting the head and feet off a chicken with a small hatchet. A cigarette hung on his lower lip, ash trembling with every blow. Scooping up claws and head, he rattled them into a metal bucket, expertly trussed the carcass with twine and hung it from a hook.

Rachel moved on. At a fruit stall she reached an apple off the top of a shiny, red pyramid. "*Sei,*" she said to the woman behind the counter. "And six oranges, *per favore.*"

Next, a stand covered with great wheels of yellow and white cheeses. Willow baskets piled with brown and white speckled eggs driven in that morning from outlying rural districts lined a ledge behind the stall. She bought a dozen, some cheese, then bread, a bottle of red wine, one of water, coffee and a small bouquet of roses at successive stalls. Her shopping bag was heavy when she left the market, bumping against her shins as she emerged into the street. In her other hand she held the flowers, blooms down.

It had cleared during the afternoon, grown bitter. The sky, a dark inky blue perceptibly deepening to black, seemed closer somehow, more tangible than in Manhattan where true darkness was held off by neon and the funneling of skyscrapers. Here it was rich as

33

spangled velvet, the stars hardening to magnesium white. Lamps set over doorways and on corners mellowed the gunmetal gray of the cobbles, gilding the earth tones of buildings to gold. Through open shutters Rachel glimpsed a stuccoed ceiling, pendant crystal chandelier winking in firelight, and at ground level, a desk set against the window, lamp angled low over an open book. She heard a dog bark, a baby cry, and on the air caught a waft of cigar smoke drifting from a balcony, the mutter of male voices. By the time she reached the lane where her apartment was located, it was completely dark.

Calmed by the day's work and weary from walking, Rachel's hand was on the latch when a high-pitched whine sounded behind her. A scooter whizzed by, barely missing, swerved, wheels leaning perilously close to the ground then, impossibly, righted itself. The rider shouted something, words churning into the squeal of engine. Then he was gone. She was still looking after him when a hand clamped around her wrist. She swung round, twisting instinctively, her shoulder wrenching from the hands clawing at the straps of her bags. Breath on her face, the sheen of saliva over teeth, a curse. Locked in an obscene embrace, Rachel fought back, grappling her assailant like a demented lover. Fortyish face, pouchy beneath the eyes, he had fingers with a strength so absolute, so alien, it threatened to crush her spirit like foil. A shutter opened. "What's going on?" a voice called. Suddenly she was alone, intact, stupid with shock.

Blindly Rachel felt for her purse and satchel. Still there. Only her shopping bag lay on the ground, disgorging its contents. The cheese had tumbled out of its wrapper and was beginning to sweat, two of the eggs were oozing a gelatinous mess that made her gag. The flowers lay trampled, petals strewn about the street. She knelt, shoved the cheese into the bag, and without thinking, began to gather up the flowers. Her stomach gave a single violent lurch.

Abandoning the flowers, she flung open the gate, ran up the steps and stumbled through the door into her apartment.

V

THE WATER IN THE BOWL SWIRLED CLOUDY, then clear. The handle of the toilet snapped up. Rachel leaned against the bathroom wall, a towel pressed to her lips. Roses swam in her vision like blobs in a lava lamp, blearing, elongating, detaching, endlessly cycling, oily and heavy as blood. She leaned over the tub and turned the faucets on full. Her hands, so implacable, so steady a few moments ago, shook uncontrollably. The roar of water filled her ears.

She was back again in the room.

It lay deep within an abandoned house at the heart of a great park. Wallpaper, blackened at the edges, streaked with water stains, its pattern still discernible in places, clung to bubbling plaster and rotten lathe. Tiny red flowers climbing a trellis of gold. She stood with her back to her stepfather and traced them with her fingertips. That was when she felt his hands upon her.

The bath was full. Rachel undressed slowly, almost ritually, dropping her clothes one by one. Then she stepped in and lay down, holding her arms stiffly by her sides, knees drawn up and loosely apart.

Just so he had positioned her.

She did not struggle, nor cry out. Instead she turned her head to the wall and fixed her eyes upon the roses. At his touch she began to count.

One, two . . .

Spread-eagled on the trellis, reds churning and shifting around her.

One hundred . . .

And as the water moved over and under her, lifting, rocking, she knew herself betrayed.

One hundred and forty-four.

When Rachel roused herself the water in the bath was cold. She reached for a towel and stood up. Gouts of water slithered down her thighs into the mouth of the drain. She began to weep, a raw, flayed sound, without tears.

She had been fourteen. One hundred and forty-four stood for fourteen years and four months. That hadn't taken her long to figure out. She'd always been good at math.

Later, combing her hair before the fire she asked herself the old question. Why hadn't she resisted?

The comb snagged. She yanked at it, punishing herself. The knot suddenly gave way, teeth sliding through to the ends, grazing her shoulder.

The answer was as familiar as the scent of her own skin.

She had trusted him.

A young girl, rocking on a frontporch swing, waiting for her mother to come home. The paint on the window sill next to her arm was cracked, blistered, and she picked at it with her fingernails while she read from the book balanced on her thighs.

She couldn't remember the story but she remembered white flakes fluttering down, littering the porch, sticking to the soles of her feet whenever the arc of the swing brought them close enough to brush the floor. They had felt prickly, hot from the sun striping the boards.

Suddenly her head snapped up, ponytail lashing her cheek. She hadn't heard him come. One moment she was alone, the next he was there. He was smiling.

Rachel took a hefty swig from her glass. The bottle was already a third down.

Her stepfather was always smiling. His teeth, white, regular, perfect. No, not quite perfect. A tiny chip on one of the front teeth at the bottom. And the way he smelled. Sweet, like fabric conditioner. And clean. After he hugged her she would look at the marks his starched collar had made on her cheek and touch them secretly. He was good to her. Sometimes he gave her money.

She trusted him.

But today was different. He wasn't wearing a tie, the top two buttons of his shirt were undone and his blazer hung over his shoulder, his thumb hooked through the label. He was looking at her, blue eyes slitting against the glare. Movie star eyes. Sapphires fringed with gold. She remembered how the air held its breath, how the wind chimes stilled. She held his gaze, willing him to say something, anything, so the world could get on.

"Let's go for a walk," he said. "There's something I want you to see."

Roses.

She had seen them. Touched them.

But when she started to count they were no longer flowers but bursts of blood splattering against stone. Like the kid on a bike in her neighborhood who'd been hit by a truck, the wheels still spinning when her schoolbus pulled up alongside.

Rachel wiped her mouth with the back of her hand and refilled her glass.

That's how it had been in the clinic afterwards when she knew, when her mother knew.

Five months pregnant. She sat there seeing wheels turning, rust stains on blacktop, a candy wrapper, horrifying commonplaces.

"Rachel." Behind glinting lenses the doctor's eyes looked opaque. Dark hairs matted the back of his hands, tufted out the top of his collar. A steel instrument poked out of the breast pocket of his lab coat. Then her mother's face, powder caking in creases, lipstick smudged, caved in. Rachel saw something in her eyes, a restless animal, but didn't know what.

"How do we get rid of it?" her mother said.

Later, Rachel heard the nurses whispering. There were complications, she had lost a lot of blood, they were keeping her overnight for observation. It was late afternoon when they wheeled her to a room and put her in a bed next to a window. It looked out onto the jumble of the Manhattan skyline with the December sun sliding down behind in a welter of red. In front, the blinds dissected the room into long strips.

A huge bloody rose against a lattice of black.

That was when she started screaming.

Rachel nudged the bottle with her foot wondering if she could handle another glass on an empty stomach. She looked at her watch. Only nine-thirty. Better make coffee.

She was spooning grounds into a filter when there was a rap on the door. For a moment she thought the man in the alley had returned. "Who is it?" Her voice was brittle, not hers.

"Donati."

Padding across the floor with bare feet, she opened the door against the chain, one hand clutching her robe at the neck.

"Hi." He was holding a manila envelope. "I brought the report."

"Oh." She'd forgotten. "Thanks."

He hesitated, still holding the envelope. "Do you mind if I come in?"

Reluctantly, Rachel unhooked the chain. The door felt heavy, enormous. She left him to let himself in and returned to the kitchen. She heard the door close, felt his eyes on her. She pressed the on button on the coffeemaker and sat down again on the floor by the fire, legs tucked under, robe tight around her knees, head down and averted so her hair shielded her face.

He was still standing in the middle of the floor. She could feel him taking in the room; groceries lying unpacked on the countertop, cabinet doors left open, the wine glass. She began to run the comb through her hair again. She felt drugged, erased. She didn't care if he thought she was drunk.

"Are you OK?"

"Fine." She nodded at the bottle. "Want some?"

"No thanks."

"Have a seat."

They sat in silence, the only noise the gurgle of the coffeemaker and hiss of the gas. "I'll get it," Donati said after a while. He moved to the kitchen, found two mugs and poured the coffee. The rush of liquid, a spoon chinking against ceramic. "Cream, sugar?"

"Black."

He came round the counter and held out a cup.

"Thanks." She put it down on the floor beside her, untasted.

"Are you sure you're all right?" he asked again.

"Jetlag." Rachel divided her hair into hanks and began to plait it, soothed by the rhythm of strand over strand. She was beginning to coalesce, reconstitute back into someone she recognized, who was recognizable to others. Securing the ends with a tieback she flung the braid over her shoulder. *When he finishes his coffee*, she thought, *I'll ask him to leave.*

VI

THE NEXT DAY, ON THE WAY TO THE MUSEUM, Rachel pondered not so much the results of Donati's tests which were what she had expected after her cursory examination of the triptych the day before, but his discovery several weeks ago that Persegati and the Eliot-Simpson Museum in Manhattan had ordered a private examination of the triptych not more than a month before Rachel was given the assignment. The results indicated the triptych was very possibly a lost work by Rogier Van der Weyden. Rachel heard the name like a suckerpunch to the gut. Rogier was one of the two most celebrated Northern Renaissance painters, the other being Jan van Eyck, and the discovery of a lost masterpiece by him was a career-making, once-in-a-lifetime event. Suspicion instantly replaced elation. Why had this been kept from her?

As soon as Donati left she picked up the phone and dialed New York. She was told the curator was in a meeting. Dissatisfied, she left a message.

Up until two, pacing back and forth, going over and over the significance of Donati's news, trying to tie in Apex's connection.

The report indicated that the painting had originated in Northern Europe and that the mix of pigments was similar to those favored in Rogier's Bruges workshop, the busy port giving more access to a wider variety of pigment than in Brussels. Donati's own tests confirmed this. But Rachel was acutely aware of how tenuous all this was. Despite the accuracy of the initial carbon 14 dating that put the triptych somewhere in the first half of the fifteenth century, the painter would remain unknown until the figures on the panel could be uncovered. But she could make no sense of Apex's involvement, and Persegati's. By five-thirty in the morning, she had made the decision to confront him with her knowledge of the report.

She was shown in by Persegati's assistant who told her that he had just arrived and was in his office.

"But he asked not to disturbed," she called after her as Rachel headed for the library.

"Slept well?" she said to Venus as she passed underneath the painting. She walked down the corridor leading off the library and, after a cursory knock, went straight in.

He was sitting at his desk, a paper knife hovering over a pile of letters in front of him. If he was irritated at her abrupt appearance he didn't show it. He laid down the knife and stood up.

"Dr. Piers, you are early. What a pleasant surprise!" He gestured to a chair. "Coffee?"

"Please." Anything to clear her head. The events of the night before as well as the wine on an empty stomach, had left her with a powerful emotional hangover.

Punching an intercom, Persegati spoke into it, then laid his hands on the arms of his chair, a medieval king about to give judgment, the gleam of a heavy gold signet ring on the little finger of his right hand completing the effect.

"You have something to say before the meeting?"

"Yes. Two things actually. One concerns the fact that you ordered an initial examination of the triptych, the results of which were kept from me and my team. And second, exactly what has Apex to do with this project? Satisfy me on these two points and there's a chance I won't be on the next plane back to New York."

The assistant entered carrying a tray. The cups and saucers of fine china smattered about the rim with tiny blue flowers—forget-me-nots or cornflowers—rattled delicately as she set the tray down on the desk. Very English, very feminine, and totally at odds with the almost overbearing sparseness of the room. But not, Rachel was coming to realize, with Persegati's tastes.

The assistant poured the coffee in a thin, dark stream, bruising the flowers to violet through the wafer transparency of the china. When the cups were full she handed one to Persegati and then one to Rachel. The assistant's movements were efficient to the point of abrupt and some of the coffee slopped into the saucer and splashed onto Rachel's skirt.

"Thank you, Anna. If Dr. Thompson and the others arrive, would you kindly ask them to wait in the library?"

She nodded and turned to leave.

"And Anna? I am expecting an important call from the monsignor at the Vatican museums, so please put it through as soon as it comes in."

"Very good, Dr. Persegati."

He studied his coffee cup for some moments. Its arrival had given him time to compose himself.

"I am, as you know, the director of the Roman State Institute for Conservation. In such capacity, I really have two jobs. One . . ." he lifted a carefully manicured finger, "I am responsible for the conservation of this city's artifacts. But, as you are doubtless aware, that cannot be done without money." He came round the front of the desk and topped up Rachel's cup then leaned against the edge of the desk with his arms folded and chin down as if inspecting the tips of his shoes. The weak January sunlight glossed his oiled hair and picked out a burgundy thread in the weave of his suit.

"Which brings me to the second point. I am a fund-raiser, Dr. Piers. A business man, if you will. As you are no doubt aware, without capital we cannot preserve our national treasures. It is my practice to conduct a preliminary analysis before going ahead with conservation. Depending on the results I then go to a certain individual or corporation and ask for sponsorship. In this case, I approached the Apex Corporation, which, as you may know, owns factories in Italy."

Rachel shook her head. "No, I didn't know. So when you thought the triptych could be a lost work of Rogier Van der Weyden you knew you could go after a big sponsor, like Fujifilm and the Sistine Chapel," she said.

Persegati sighed. "That is not the way I would have put it, Dr. Piers, but essentially, that is correct. Big business. . . . How can I say this delicately?" His hands fluttered in the air. "Big business prefers big names."

"In return for what, might I ask?"

He walked around his desk as if he wanted to put himself out of range of her questions.

"Media rights?" She was fishing pretty wildly but she knew she must have snagged at something when she saw a look of irritation pass over his face.

"Dr. Piers, please do not think I have completely sold my soul to the devil. That is not the Italian way. We prefer something altogether more . . . *indirect,* let us say."

"I understand." Fujifilm had agreed to sponsor the restoration of Michelangelo's fading masterpiece in return for exclusive film rights to the process. It had netted them enormous international prestige.

"In addition to paying for the restoration process, the Apex Corporation will buy the exclusive rights to sponsor an international exhibition in Tokyo, London, and New York should the triptych prove to be a Rogier. That exhibition will begin here at this museum and finish up at the Eliot-Simpson."

That would be quite a coup, Rachel had to admit. And clever of him. The museum would get the media coverage without seeming to directly solicit it. Donati had been right and wrong at the same time. Apex would profit from the triptych but it was nothing so crude as money. Their name would be splashed all over the exhibition, and her own museum would share in the glory. Obviously that was the key to her own involvement.

Without hesitation she said, "My position here is compromised."

"I don't follow."

"Authenticating the triptych as a Rogier is clearly in my own interests, and that of my museum."

"Actually, the Apex Corporation specifically requested your involvement. They are *extremely* optimistic about your ability to authenticate it correctly. As I am, I assure you."

"Nevertheless." Rachel placed her cup and saucer on the desk and stood up.

"We did not want to prejudice your work by telling you beforehand," he said in a more conciliatory tone.

"That hasn't been a problem before. Besides, the work's either by Rogier or it isn't. Either way, the job's the same."

"Quite so, Dr. Piers. I admire your, how you say, rectitude."

Rachel didn't see that morality had anything to do with it. What concerned her was her professional integrity. She marveled at Persegati's obtuseness, feigned or real she couldn't tell.

"What will happen to the triptych afterwards?" Rachel asked. "Providing, of course, it turns out to be a Rogier. And if it isn't a Rogier?"

Just then the phone rang.

"Ah, Monsignor. Just a moment, if you please." Persegati put his hand over the mouthpiece. "I beg you to give some thought to what I have said. We would be desolated to lose your expertise on what may prove to be an historic project."

VII

SEVERAL HOURS LATER, Rachel was back in her apartment making coffee. She had returned to check her messages and e-mails. Nothing. She dialed her New York curator at home but got his answering machine.

Lifting the lid of the trash can to throw in the coffee grounds she saw the cheese with the roses lying on top. She flung in the brown grit and let the lid drop.

Filling her mug, she carried it to an armchair in the living room and studied Donati's report, paying particular attention to the condition of the frame with a view to the risk of unbolting it from the wall and transferring it to the lab. As far as she could tell there was no absolute reason why the triptych couldn't be restored in the chapel. Her previous objections to the church as the site of restoration began to seem unreasonable, especially when she recalled that Persegati seemed eager to transfer it from the church to the lab as soon as possible. His motives were less to do with the good of the triptych, Rachel knew, than the appearance of ownership. By the time she had discovered who the painter was the congregation would have become accustomed to its absence.

It was not surprising, therefore, that when she announced in the meeting she intended to restore the triptych on site, Persegati seemed jumpy.

"Surely," he said. "The job could be done more efficiently in the laboratory?"

"Maybe," she replied. "But by the time we get the frame wrapped in linen and moved, we'll have wasted precious time. Of course, we *could* move it to the lab, but it would add three weeks to the schedule." She looked round at the others for confirmation.

"Unless the frame disintegrates and we have to piece it back together," Donati said. "Then we're looking at a couple of months."

"At least," Rachel added. "We'd better plan on June or July at the earliest to be on the safe side."

Persegati was standing at the window with his back to them during this exchange. "Dr. Thompson?"

In reality, Nigel was a more senior member of the team than Rachel. An acknowledged expert in his field, he had published several books on frame restoration and was an authority on Vermeer and the seventeenth century Dutch school of painters. Although only part of the team in an advisory role, Rachel knew his approbation was crucial. She was relying on the fact that Donati had told him of Persegati's end run around the team.

"Considering the panels are structurally sound and that the move itself might damage them, let alone the frame. . . ." His lips moved silently as if he were running equations in his head.

In the interval between meetings she had thought through her argument very carefully, aware that Nigel would judge it entirely on its technical merits. She could almost hear his mental cogs turning and meshing.

"Given the time period," he said out loud. "The frame's probably nailed or glued onto the panels, then covered with gesso, *bole,* gold leaf, so it's pretty solid. Not really a border so much as an extension of the panels themselves. If it's oak, so much the better. As Dr. Piers says, what we would lose in the inconvenience of restoring it on site, we would save in time."

Rachel turned to the tense silhouette at the window. "Dr. Persegati?" She could sense that he too was weighing location versus timing. From their conversation that morning she knew the sooner the triptych was identified the better.

"Very well," he said.

"Do you want me to square it with Brother Angelo?" Donati asked after the others had left.

"The monsignor should certainly be told. I don't see what Angelo's got to do with it."

"It would be a kindness."

Rachel shrugged.

"By the way," Donati said as they were leaving the museum. "Can you meet me at the lab later on?"

"Sure," Rachel replied. "When?"

"About four."

It was only after she had got back to her apartment that she realized that he hadn't told her the address.

It was after twelve when Rachel left her apartment for the second time that day. She had exchanged her suit for jeans, baggy sweater, sneakers, baseball cap, and a denim jacket, the quintessential American tourist. She needed to think but her apartment was beginning to make her claustrophobic, fifteen paces from wall to wall, then back again.

She stopped to take her bearings and realized that she was standing in the exact spot where the scooter had erupted the night before. She tugged the peak of her cap lower down. For good measure, she added sunglasses.

Ten minutes later, she came out into a busy street with a pedestrian bridge directly in front of her. The squat fortress of the Castel Sant'Angelo reared up at the opposite end, a type of medieval "Checkpoint Charlie" dividing the city on one side and Vatican City on the other. It was here, at the Bridge of Angels, that the sacred and the profane had trysted for centuries. Through the branches of the leafless trees lining the river, the dome of St. Peter's rose massive and dominating, lording it over the skyline.

Hovering on the edge of the curb, she waited for the light to change. Once across she walked towards the center of the bridge, now empty of the African street vendors who hawked leather goods to tourists in the summer. She stopped and leaned over the stone balustrade.

The river glinted gray in the winter sunshine, its surface glassy until puckered and ribbed by the currents lurking near the massive feet of the bridge. Seabirds driven from the coastal areas by winter gales patrolled in the scum near the banks or bobbed idly in the center of the current. Rachel felt the panic of the night before begin to recede like an outgoing tide. Digging her chin deeper into the collar of her jacket she hugged her arms about her for warmth. This morning had found her cast up on the shore like some latter-day Robinson Crusoe, her only choice to pick through the wreckage and decide what was necessary for survival, and what was not.

In an odd way she was grateful for the complications surrounding the triptych. They allowed her to be wholly preoccupied, while a membrane grew back over the past.

Now she knew it wasn't for her expertise in conservation as much as for her relative naiveté of what went on behind the scenes of a major Manhattan museum that she had been picked for this assignment. A technician rather than a bureaucrat, she was the ideal person to get the job done without asking awkward questions. If the triptych turned out to be a Rogier, there was little chance she could prevent it from becoming a permanent exhibit in a museum, rather than being left in relative obscurity in the church.

A stone angel, one of a series sculpted by Bellini when he overhauled the bridge in the 1600s, rose into the sky next to her shoulder. A swatch of cloth fell in folds over the angel's arms and down its legs, bare almost to the thighs. Rachel felt cold just looking at it. The last time she had seen it was four years ago in a sweltering ninety-five degrees. Then she had envied its near nakedness.

Wings partially folded and drooping at the tips, its expression enigmatic, a hint of a smile tugging at the corners of the mouth despite the mournful stance, Rachel could never figure out the joke. An ambulance tore up the Lungotevere Castello heading for the hospital of Santo Spirito in Sassia on the opposite side of the Tiber, its siren shrill, alien. Abandoning the bridge she plunged back into the labyrinth of streets.

When she came to the piazza in front of the church, she found a group of old men gathered there on the steps of the fountain to gossip and to smoke. In front of the others, a few pigeons looking at him with hooded eyes, one of the men stood in perfect mimicry of a classic bowling stance with the fingers of his right hand splayed around an imaginary ball. Then he shuffled two steps and loosened his grip.

The imaginary ball came sweetly to a stop, rocking from side to side until it became perfectly still. His audience was riveted. Even the pigeons cocked their heads on one side as if calculating the trajectory of the throw.

The winning shot.

The crowd, such as it was, went wild. One old man tapped his stick vigorously on the side of the fountain, another hoisted an imaginary glass while the others raised a hoarse cheer. The victor bowed gravely, fished a cigarette from behind his ear, placed it in the corner of his mouth, then patted his pockets for matches. The birds resumed their strutting.

The show was over.

Rachel crossed the square. The doors under the portico were unlocked, the church deserted, quiet. She walked down the central aisle, past the saints on their cornices, past the candles. The air was scented with the smoke that rose like gossamer from their wavering tips. Then she stopped.

A voice could be heard in the chapel, so low as to be almost undetectable. Walking softly now, she came to the iron grille that divided the chapel from the church and looked in.

Brother Angelo knelt before the altar, hands gripping the ledge of the prie dieu, sandaled feet kicking childishly out behind him. A string of jet beads spilled over the edge of the chair. A silver cross swung from the end of the rosary, catching the gold of the candle flames, flashing it back in white arcs. Gold to silver. Reverse alchemy.

In the half-light of the chapel, Angelo's cassock looked ghostly. His prayers rose and fell like some childish chant in a game. She could make out only one word, endlessly repeated.

"*Madonna*," he said. "*Madonna*."

"Angelo," Rachel said. "It's me."

At the sound of her voice he leapt off the kneeler, shielding the triptych with his body.

"No take her!" Angelo shouted. "She belong to me."

Donati walked into the chapel.

"Tell her," Angelo said to Donati.

"What are you doing here?" asked Rachel, irritably. Angelo's attachment to the triptych spooked her, made her feel a responsibility for him that threatened her professional objectivity.

"You told me to ask the monsignor permission to turn the chapel into a work site," Donati said. "Plus, I realized I hadn't given you the address of the lab."

VIII

Donati insisted walking would take them less time than a taxi. It was rush hour and the roads were clogged, so it sounded reasonable enough. Only when they had been walking for half an hour, did Rachel begin to have second thoughts.

She was about to protest that she could go no further when he stopped in front of what looked like a derelict warehouse.

Donati was already opening the door. He led her up a flight of concrete steps. "Most of the other labs have been moved to a new building," he explained. "But I prefer to work here."

He patted the metal railing where the paint had blistered and flaked off, leaving patches of exposed metal that had rusted to a deep oxide red. They looked like sores that refused to heal. "It's due to be demolished in a few months." They had come to a landing with double doors facing them.

Inside, a huge space seemed to take up the entire third floor. A row of windows ran the length of one side and there were skylights in the ceiling but so dirty and patterned with dead leaves that Rachel thought it would be a miracle if they let any light in at all. The rapidly waning light outside rendered them doubly superfluous but at least, she noted, they were all intact. They must be at the top of the building.

"Are you the only one who works here?" Rachel asked. She had expected to see several white-coated technicians moving quietly about their stations. Instead, apart from themselves, the lab was deserted.

"A couple of other die-hards," Donati replied. "But I told them they could go home early. There's a soccer match against Naples tonight, and they were making stupid mistakes. Too keyed up to concentrate."

Glancing rapidly around, Rachel saw that the room contained an odd mixture of old-fashioned and state of the art equipment. There was a hot table for stretching canvases, a colorimeter for measuring and specifying colors, and next to it a fumigation cabinet for destroying mold, and a low-pressure suction table for attaching linings to canvas for the purpose of reinforcement. Off to the side was a row of computers, turned off, except for one where a white cursor blinked against a row of numbers on a green screen.

A kerosene stove stood in the middle of the floor, heroically beating back the drafts that eddied around the floor and ceiling, alternately sucking and blowing at her ankles and face like huge icy exhalations.

"It's a little chilly," Donati admitted. "But you get used to it." As if to prove the point, he took off his jacket and tossed it onto a chair. Then he bent to retrieve something from his coat pocket.

"Should you be doing that in here?" Rachel indicated the Bunsen burners and conical flasks, some of them filled with what looked like highly flammable liquids. A large cork-stoppered bottle sporting the label "diacetone alcohol" confirmed it. A No Smoking sign hung from one screw on the wall behind him. He shrugged and waved the extinguished match towards a bench.

"It's over there."

A huge black microscope was sitting in lordly isolation on the countertop, alone except for a scattering of glass slides around its base and a row of test tubes lined up along a wooden stand behind it. Besides this, and a few sheets of paper covered in Donati's handwriting, there was little else. Rachel instantly recognized the labels on the test tubes; samples from the triptych.

Donati leaned over the eyepiece of the microscope, adjusting the focus.

"Take a look at this," he said, making room.

At first Rachel could only make out vague smudges of brown. She fiddled with the focus, her fingers clumsy with cold. Suddenly, what had looked before like a cardboard box left out in the rain, all smushed edges and brown pulp, sharpened into a complex strata of lines running bilaterally across the slide, speckled here and there by spherical blotches.

"It's part of the frame."

"See anything else?"

The lines looked enigmatically back at her, mocking her from their vantage point of great antiquity.

"Maybe a few traces of oil or gesso, probably splashes from the panels."

"Linseed oil and gum arabic," said Donati. "I also found traces of parchment glue and plaster of Paris."

Rachel nodded. The latter mixture would be the gesso, a coating used to prepare the panels for the application of the paint. The former must be the emulsion medium for the oils. *Gum tempera.* Rachel knew that paints so mixed rendered a brilliant translucent finish and were prized by medieval artists, but they had a notoriously low tolerance to damp and poor conditions. She thought of the blooms she had seen on the panels, the result of "inherent vice" in the materials.

"If the first report's correct and the triptych originated in Northern Europe," she said, squinting harder. "It must be some sort of hardwood. Walnut, oak maybe."

"Guess again."

Rachel raised her head. "What do you mean?"

"See those striations running from the top left hand corner diagonally across the slide?"

Rachel turned back to the eyepiece.

"That's one of the telltale signs of softwood," Donati went on. "It's probably poplar or pine. I sent a sample to another lab for independent corroboration. When it comes back we'll have its exact genus."

Rachel stared at it until the lines began to dissolve and merge into each other. Of course. That was the only thing that could explain the damage to the frame. It must have been made in Italy. But if the panels were painted in Northern Europe, why not simply frame it there? It didn't make sense. Even back then it was commonly known that the hardwoods indigenous to the colder climates were more resistant to the forces of time and nature than the softer woods of the Mediterranean.

The "inherent vice" factor of poplar and pine was far greater than that of oak. In addition, the concept of a frame functioning more as a border than an integral part of the overall design was a later historical development when art salons became popular and the pieces were moved for display. Before that, art was a more permanent fixture intended primarily for religious and civic devotion.

"Is it possible the painting originated here?"

Donati shook his head. "Nope. The initial report and my own tests have conclusively placed it in Northern Europe. The panels are made of oak and accounts for the fact that there's very little structural damage." He skimmed through the row of slides, selected one and held it up. "This, for instance, is 'dragon's blood.' I know it's one of the most commonly used faux pigments since Roman times and it was used all over Europe. But . . ."

"It was used predominantly in manuscript illumination, *not* in panel painting," Rachel said. Pia would know more about this than she. She took the slide and held it up to the light. The flecks on the glass did indeed look like traces of dried blood. No wonder Pliny the Elder had propagated the myth that it derived from the blood of dragons and elephants commingled in the crucible of battle. The truth was far less exotic: it derived from the resin of a species of palm that flourished in Asia. Still, the spurious name had a romantic ring to it that bespoke a time when anything was believable provided it could be worked into a story. Better by far, she had always thought, than the pared down utility and techno-wizardry of the present day with its endless catalog of abstractions and molecular structures. "And most of the significant illumination was executed in Northern Europe at this time," she said.

"Correct."

Rachel put the slide back on the counter as carefully as if it had been a sacred relic.

"All right then." She took a blank sheet of paper from the bench and began jotting down notes. "This is what we know. One, the initial tests suggest Flemish origin. And your results certainly seem to confirm a general location of Northern Europe. Two, the frame originates here, which is highly unusual considering the smallish size of the triptych, but which certainly explains the damage."

Donati lit another cigarette, regarding her thoughtfully through the smoke.

"Let's assume it was commissioned specifically for the church. Let's also assume it was painted in Bruges."

"Not Brussels?"

"Not necessarily. That's where Van der Weyden's main workshop was but he also had one in Bruges. His most gifted apprentice, Hans Memling, studied at Bruges. Anyway, we won't know for sure until I get a look at the style. But Northern Europe for sure." Rachel tapped the pen against her teeth, staring into space. "OK, so let's assume it was made there but was always intended for Rome. Perhaps it was cheaper to frame here. Unlikely, but who knows? In any case, that means Pia can probably dig something up at the church as they usually listed any gifts received, especially if it entailed prayers for the donor."

"A sort of spiritual bribe." Donati flicked his ash into a trash can near his feet.

"Something like that," Rachel acknowledged. "Or maybe it was a gift. No strings attached. In which case, it'll be harder to track." She got down from the stool and walked towards the door. "It's a start," she said. "But it isn't enough."

"You'll have to wait." Donati had already begun switching off lights, gradually reducing the room to a series of indistinct shapes bathed by the orange glow of the dying stove. The benches looked like hobos huddled around a brazier, reminding Rachel of some of the seedier sections of New York—the Bronx, Hell's Kitchen. "All I can give you now are the results from the x-rays." He tossed her a dossier. "The usual layers; gesso, no *bosso* . . ."

Bosso, or red clay, was commonly used as a ground for gold leaf. Its absence meant there was no gold leaf on the actual panels, only on the frame. Replacing it was finicky, time-consuming and expensive, requiring patience and the lightest of touches in applying the wafers of gold.

" . . . oil paint, a thin coating of varnish. That's the lot."

"No sign of later conservation attempts?"

"None."

"Good," Rachel said. "That's one headache we won't have to worry about. Once we get rid of the dirt layer we'll be down to the original pigments. What about the infra-red tests? Any under-modeling, signature?"

"I haven't gotten around to that yet."

"Tomorrow we'll set up a raking light so I can see if there's any damage to the surface of the panels."

IX

THEY LEFT THE BUILDING and Rachel waited while Donati locked up. Night had fallen and the street lamps threw pointed shadows along the wall of the building like gigantic fragments of splintered glass.

"Let's get a drink," Donati said, pocketing the key.

When they reached the station he veered off from the direction of the taxi stands and stopped at a bar occupying one of the squared corners of the *Stazione Termini*, Rome's main train terminal.

The bar's interior looked as if it knew that its customers came only to fortify themselves so they would have sufficient strength to move on to more agreeable surroundings—cheap patio chairs, mismatched, a streaked mirror advertising a liqueur Rachel had never heard of, a few postcards tacked onto the wall, lopsided. A scattering of yellowing Formica-topped tables took up most of the cramped floor space. An elderly man with gray stubble on his chin was polishing glasses at a counter that fronted a meagerly stocked bar. Behind him an espresso machine steamed and gurgled busily as if it prided itself on being the only significant sign of life in the place.

Except for a man sitting in the corner with a newspaper held in front of his face, the place was empty of customers. A mute TV sagged from a metal bracket above the bar, throwing out a kaleidoscope of dislocated images while a row of buzzing fluorescent lights supplied the missing background noise. Donati began to chat with the man behind the counter and Rachel studied him covertly as she massaged the back of her neck with her fingertips. When he turned away from the bar, she dropped her gaze. The next moment he put a glass in front of her and raised his own to his lips. "*Salute!*"

"*Salute!*"

Campari; carmine red and laced with bitter herbs beneath the surface sweetness, but somehow the opposites managed to coexist without canceling each other out.

"Is that OK?" asked Donati.

"It's great. Thanks."

He stretched back in his chair. "*Bene.*"

"Is this your local?" Rachel asked.

"Not really." He nodded towards the bar. "Gino's a friend."

"You seem to know everyone in this town."

"'Town?' You make it sound almost neighborly."

"It's one of the enduring myths that Americans still get all choked up about. It makes us feel safe, as if people really cared about each other." She nodded at the man reading the newspaper. "There are other ways to do it, though. Take that guy over there, for instance."

The man crossed his legs as if conscious of their gaze, his trousers hitching up at the ankle to reveal an inch of navy silk above expensive shoes. He turned a page of the newspaper and a gold watch flashed at his wrist.

Donati barely glanced at him. Instead, he leaned towards her with his elbows on the table. "Tell me. Do *you* feel safe?"

For a moment she panicked, thinking he must have guessed what had happened the night before. "Not really," she said at last, recalling the craziness she saw everyday in the New York subway; the hands held out, the faces beseeching, intimidating, the palpable resentment.

All this time she had been unconsciously tracing her glass along the lines of fake marbling in the plastic of the table as if seeking a way out of the question, but they kept spiraling back on themselves, bringing her back to where she started. Now she looked up. "After 9/11 I'm not sure anyone feels safe anymore. Do you?"

"Personally?" he said. "Sure. Generally, not a chance. Take Gino, for instance. He owned a cafe near the Jewish Ghetto for twenty years, did great business. He knew all the regulars, most of them friends. Then the zoning laws kicked in and the property along his street was condemned. So he moved here, hoping to reclaim some of his losses by the guaranteed clientele at the station. Now look at him."

Rachel realized that the man was re-wiping glasses he had already cleaned as if the bar were some infernal circle of hell, and he was doomed to repeat himself over and over again.

"I come in from time to time." Donati finished the dregs in his glass and held it up, rotating it slowly. "In this city, apart from the bars, the churches are one of the few places left where people can still feel community, can still feel as if they belong."

The man across from them tossed a few coins onto the table beside the newspaper. The crumpled pages rose in the draft from the closing door like a hand languidly waving good-bye.

"Tell me." Rachel leaned forward over the table "Is this why you brought me here? To lecture me on the evils of capitalism, the virtues of the working man?" Deliberately provoking him, Rachel wanted to see what lay beneath the composure, how seriously he took himself.

"I thought it worth a shot," he smiled.

Relieved, Rachel sat back and regarded him over the rim of her glass. "Nigel warned me you were idealistic but I had no idea."

Donati didn't respond. He pulled out a small leather pouch and Rachel watched as he extracted a leaf of paper from one side and a quantity of tobacco from the other. He crumbled the brown flakes evenly over the center of the paper as if carefully laying a gunpowder trail, then rolling the edges of the paper together between thumb and forefinger, he ran the tip of his tongue along one side to seal it. After tapping it lightly on his wrist, he held it up to her, his eyes questioning.

She shook her head.

"Suit yourself." Donati put it to his lips, fumbling for matches. His eyes narrowed as the end caught. "My father worked in the slaughterhouse."

Rachel gave a small start, expecting politics, not autobiography. It was like his offering her one of his own rolled cigarettes instead of a Marlboro.

A thin stream of smoke trickled from his lips. "I grew up in the working class district of the *Testaccio*. You know it?"

"I've heard of it," Rachel replied, intrigued. "The area known in the Middle Ages as the *Prati del Popolo Romano* (Meadow of the Roman People)?"

The *Testaccio* district was famous now for its defunct gasometer, a huge cylindrical structure that loomed above the rows of tenements and warehouses like the skeleton of an ancient watchtower. From what she remembered, it had been considered the chief success of the People's Block Government because it had assured Rome an independent energy supply. As soon as the city had been converted to underground gas, it had been rendered obsolete. When this happened, the slaughter-houses had become the main source of revenue for the district. She was beginning to understand now why Donati had taken this tack. He had grown up in the shadow of one of Rome's greatest socialist symbols.

"I was the youngest of nine," Donati continued. "You know, one of those teeming Catholic families. We did all right, though. That is, until 1980. I was ten. That was when the government decided to build a more modern facility out of town. Overnight, they laid off hundreds of workers, my father and older brothers among them. And when they applied for work at the new plant they were told that their jobs could be done more efficiently by machines."

He refilled their glasses.

"I was the only one to go to the University. My father supported me. He said that, unlike him, maybe I could make something of my life. It was at the University that

I joined the Communist Party, but I got disillusioned with the violence. So I joined various socialist factions that specialized in peaceful protest."

"What kind of protests?" Only a few weeks before, a bomb had gone off in an art gallery in the center of Rome, reducing over thirty Classical sculptures to a heap of rubble. She'd read about it in the *New York Times*. As yet, no one had claimed responsibility, although the Mafia was suspected, owing to the recent success of the current Roman District Attorney.

"Sit-ins, demonstrations, debates . . ." Donati replied. "The usual."

"Not violence?"

Donati looked at her gravely over the top of his glass. "I told you, that's not my style. I'm more interested in conservation. You know, *saving* things from destruction."

"But why conservation?"

"Art is one of the few things left that is held in common. It belongs to everyone. That's why it's imperative the triptych stays in the church. It belongs there."

She had been playing with a tear in the plastic tabletop, avoiding his gaze, the candor with which he spoke, his passion. Now she looked up. "Be realistic," she said. "This could be one of the greatest art finds this century. Apex isn't going to let a Rogier Van der Weyden slip through its fingers, not when they can take credit for its discovery." Hating herself, forcing herself to say what had been on her mind since Donati informed her about the first report.

Then she saw herself in front of the Baultenheimer Altarpiece, the cameras popping in front of her face. Working in the museum labs, she had meticulously pieced the altarpiece together like a surgeon repairing a shattered body, laboring over it with swabs, brushes and steel, uncovering and reconstructing under the piercing glare of arc lamps. For two years she accepted this as the norm. This was science at its best—clean, efficient, functional—and she was its high priestess. Then the work was completed. The patient was ready to be rehabilitated. Only then had Rachel stood back and, as if for the first time, really seen what she had done.

Faces looked back at her. Faces of angels floating in aureoles of shining hair, mouths eternally widening in a silent shout of adoration. The face of the Virgin, serene and achingly young as she clasped her infant son, oblivious of the anguish to come; the upraised eyes of the donors concealing the hope that they could yet bribe their way into heaven; and to the right, the frown of the Baptist in his rough coat of skins softened by the sweetly curving lips of St. Catherine with the wheel of her martyrdom spinning like a halo behind her, crazy with sanctity.

It was as if all the heavenly hosts had descended in one glorious and resounding "Alleluia" and caught Rachel up in its rapture. And in that moment, in that one astonished glance, she realized it was she who had conjured them back to life so they could speak again in ecstatic tongues.

Resplendently alone, it now stood in the new wing. The "jewel of the museum," the catalog called it. "A splendid example of early Renaissance technique."

Just then, Gino cleared his throat. Closing time.

Outside, the neon sign fizzed as if it were picking up static from some unknown source. Inside, Gino had begun to mop the floor with slow, deliberate strokes. Rachel lingered for a few moments, watching him.

Only a few minutes ago they had been warming themselves at his table, drinking his liquor. Now, separated by a pane of glass, it was as if he had retreated an infinite distance from them, like looking at a picture in a gallery.

"Thanks for the drink," she said to Donati as she climbed into a taxi. Unsure of how to respond to his openness about his background, Rachel's words came out brusque, even dismissive.

"Don't mention it."

He closed the door, shutting her into the dark interior of the cab. Alone once again, Rachel felt a sense of herself beginning to return. As the cab pulled away from the curb, she looked back. Double framed by the windows of the cab and the bar, she could see Gino moving about inside, tidying up. Now there were two sheets of glass separating herself and him.

And Donati?

He was somewhere in between.

X

THE BREAKTHROUGH HAD COME THE PREVIOUS WEEK. It was five o'clock, and except for a thirty minute lunch break, Rachel had spent the entire day hunched over the triptych.

She threw down the blackened swab she had been using and surveyed the panels. The accumulation of centuries of candle smoke had built up an almost impenetrable barrier against which her best efforts were proving futile. The panels looked much the same as when she had first laid eyes on them.

She scraped her stool back to get a different angle, snagging her feet in the tripod of an arc light immediately to her left. It teetered dangerously from side to side then gave one last protesting shudder before settling.

Rachel turned back to the panels. The angle of the light was all wrong. It would have to be completely realigned. She leaned in closer. There. And there.

The thick line she noticed running down the exact center of the panel when she first examined it now revealed an unmistakable texturing in the brush work.

Rachel pulled out her magnifying glass and ran it slowly over the entire length and breadth of the panel.

The line was cross-grained like wood. Not whorled and knotted like the trunk of a tree. More like the surface of planed timber, she decided. And behind it, covering the entire background, she picked out a mosaic of lozenge-shaped lines, each one connecting with the other. It was then that she knew that she was looking at a background of stones piled one on top of the other exactly like Rogier's celebrated *Crucifixion* in the Escorial.

"Look at this," she said as Donati entered the chapel.

He took the magnifying glass and bent over her shoulder.

"There," she said. "Note the difference in texture."

"*Gesu!*" Donati exclaimed. "It's the cross."

"Definitely not the *Flight into Egypt*. The mood was all wrong."

"*The Crucifixion*," Donati said. "Has to be."

"No, I don't think so." Rachel pointed to the base of the panel. "See this dark mass, it's too low. Besides, it's not centered. And there are too few figures."

He looked skeptical.

"Think about it," Rachel said. "Who do you usually get in the Crucifixion scene?" She checked them off on her fingers. "Christ's mother, Mary Magdalen, John, the soldiers, sometimes Mary, wife of Cleophas. But look. There are way too few of them. Besides, the x-rays only came up with three."

"What about the side panels?" Donati said

Rachel shook her head. "I think we'll find the donors there."

"But how can you be so sure it's not the Crucifixion?"

"I'm not." Rachel eased herself off the stool and stretched. "But personally, I put money on either *The Deposition* or *The Lamentation*."

Yesterday proved her hunch correct. The painting on the central panel was indisputably *The Lamentation*.

She and Donati had been working shoulder to shoulder when the middle figure had been identified. It was the dead Christ lying sprawled in the arms of his Mother.

It was the use of red that first tipped her off. The body was liberally bespattered around the head, hands, feet, and side like numbers in a child's dot-to-dot picture book.

"Now all we need to do is connect them up," Rachel said, "Look at this." She held out the swab she had been using; it's grimy surface was speckled with traces of red.

"'Dragon's blood'." Donati dropped it into a plastic sandwich bag, sealed it and labeled it carefully. "I'll check it later."

Rachel stared intently at the central panel. "Don't you find it odd that Rogier would use such a perishable pigment? I mean, what is one of the most accomplished painters of his time doing using a substance commonly reserved for illuminated manuscripts? He would have known that it would deteriorate almost as soon as it was dry. After all, it was intended to be used on vellum, not wood."

Donati shrugged. "No idea. Maybe it was a rush job and that's all he had to hand?"

Rachel turned towards him. "What did you just say?"

"I said, maybe it was a rush job. . . ."

"No, no," Rachel interrupted. "After that."

"Perhaps 'dragon's blood' was the only thing he could get his hands on at the time?"

"Let's go outside," she said, suddenly. "I can think better in the fresh air."

"Good," he said. "I'm dying for a smoke."

"Dying's the word. Actually, cancer," Rachel corrected over her shoulder. "One of the deadliest plagues of the twentieth century."

Outside, Rachel paced restlessly up and down the porch while Donati lit a cigarette and watched her.

"Plague," she repeated. "Plague!"

"I have no idea what you're talking about."

Rachel sat down beside him on the step. "You said that maybe 'dragon's blood' was the only thing that Rogier could get his hands on, right?"

"*Si.*"

"Well, don't you get it? It wasn't because Rogier couldn't afford the proper stuff, it was because it wasn't available."

"So?"

"Think about it. What would have made it unavailable other than an embargo at the ports? And why?"

"Plague."

"Exactly. When I was restoring a Flemish work some years ago—a contemporary of Rogier, as a matter of fact—I found out that Bruges was hit by an epidemic in the spring and summer of 1450. The port shut down—nothing coming in, nothing going out. The city was virtually in a state of siege. Now," she said. "If you were a painter with an important commission to complete, what would you do if you couldn't get the materials?"

"Use whatever was available."

"Precisely. There was always plenty of 'dragon's blood' to be had from the surrounding convents and monasteries."

"So what's the next step?"

"Pack Pia off to Bruges," said Rachel without hesitation. "And keep Nigel busy in the lab. He might turn something up that will corroborate this."

They spent the rest of the day uncovering the body of the dead Christ.

XI

THE NEXT MORNING RACHEL WASN'T SURPRISED to find the chapel empty. Eight-thirty. Donati usually didn't show up until ten. By now she had learned that Italians preferred to work later into the evening, beginning their workday midmorning, so she let it go. Besides, it made for a relatively serene walk in the morning, far different from the shoving and milling of her commute in Manhattan. Here Rachel shared the streets with elderly ladies on their way to early Mass and the slow moving but efficient auto-sweepers whose revolving brushes raked up the cigarette butts, soda cans, used bus tickets and sports pages of the day before.

Rachel liked to sit on the steps of the church and drink the coffee she bought on her way to work from the piazza's *caffe*, one of the few open at this time. She enjoyed the sounds of a city not yet fully roused, the clack of shutters as they were thrown open, the creak of clotheslines threaded through rusty grooves over alleys, the slop of water over steps accompanied by the swish,

swish of the broom wielded by the *caffe*'s owner. Most mornings a cat would come and keep her company on the steps, sprawling at her feet, regarding her with slitted, bored eyes, jumping up, suddenly feral, if Rachel attempted to pet it. Judging by its well-fed but scruffy appearance, Rachel guessed it was a stray who successfully mooched off the entire neighborhood. She had seen Angelo feeding it by the vestry door and knew that it occasionally slept in one of the confessionals if the weather was particularly cold or wet. Angelo had a name for it, but she couldn't remember what it was.

Taking down the plastic sheeting that covered the triptych she set about unpacking the equipment. The lights she would have to lug from the storeroom behind the vestry. It was time-consuming to have to clear everything away each evening but it had been one of the conditions the monsignor insisted on, that the chapel must never be locked. The church was a house of God, he said, not a laboratory. She had, however, won the argument over whether to drape opaque plastic sheeting over the iron grille dividing the chapel from the main body of the church. It would minimize dust, she argued. Besides, it was standard procedure during restorations on site. The monsignor had eventually given in. His concern, he said, was that parishioners would feel cut off from their habitual place of devotion. Better that than any harm coming to the triptych, Rachel argued. If that happened it would be moved to the lab for sure. She felt a pang as she said this, knowing that the triptych was destined to be removed from the church anyway, certain the monsignor had no inkling of this.

Now Angelo was the only one who came regularly to the chapel to pray. Rachel found traces of his presence every morning, discovering that the missal with the yellow tassels belonged to him, and every day the book was opened at a different page. During the day the plastic sheeting muffled the sounds of the church but did not keep them wholly out. Footsteps came and went, and the noonday bell would remind her to break for something to eat. Hidden from sight in the heart of the church, Rachel gradually came to feel at home there. She no longer started when Donati suddenly appeared or one of the parishioners dropped a missal in the pews. Even the creak of leather kneelers and the murmur of penitents did not disturb her as they had in the beginning. On the contrary, the muted but steady life of the church soothed her, made her feel she inhabited a context, one that was as vital as it was ordinary. It gave her a feeling that art was not to be found in museums and galleries so much as in the stuff of everyday. The hallowed silence and cool interiors of the Metropolitan Museum now seemed impersonal, dead, in contrast to the shabby but familiar interior of this church. Even her own work-station back at the Eliot-Simpson Museum in Manhattan with her photographs, post-it notes and assorted paraphernalia seemed artificial compared to this.

Angelo had also gotten used to her as if she too was becoming a familiar part of his world. He would even come into the chapel and sit at the back watching, usually in the afternoons. At first his presence disturbed her, but now it ceased to bother her. Angelo never interrupted by speaking or fidgeting, in fact she marveled at how still he could sit. Often she would straighten up to stretch and he would be gone, reminding her of the other, myriad, activities of the church; poor boxes to be emptied, fonts filled, vestments laid out in preparation for Mass. All these tasks, Angelo took great pride in.

Today, however, there was no sign of him. Crouching on the floor of the storeroom, uncoiling a length of cable that had become hopelessly tangled, Rachel heard the door to the church open and close.

"Dr. Piers?" A short, bearded man in a tan raincoat stood just outside the storeroom. He had a camera slung over his shoulder and a notepad in one hand.

"Who are you?" Rachel asked.

"Pietro Corelli, cultural editor of *Corriere della Sera*. My paper received a tip that you're about to discover a lost work of Rogier Van der Weyden. Can you verify that?"

"Afraid not." Rachel heaved a coil of cable over her shoulder and brushed past him. "I have to get this set up. So if you don't mind . . ."

"My sources are usually reliable," the man said, following her.

"Sources?"

He smiled. "It's against my paper's policy to disclose such information."

Of course. She dumped the cable onto the floor and twitched the plastic sheeting back across a gap cutting off any view of the triptych beyond and stood in front of the gate praying he wouldn't see that it was unlocked. As a place of worship the church was open to the public and, technically, he would have been within his rights to enter the chapel.

"Why the secrecy if you've got nothing to hide?" the man asked.

"Museum policy."

"Would that be the Ferrara or the Eliot-Simpson in New York?"

"You've done your homework. I'm impressed."

He ignored her jibe. "Can I at least assume that you're in charge of this project, Dr. Piers?"

"Assume anything you want," Rachel replied. "Now if you'll excuse me, I've got work to do."

She watched him walk back down the nave towards the main doors. As soon as she was sure he had gone she pulled out her cell phone.

"Pronto! Ferrara Museum."

"It's Rachel Piers. I need to speak to Dr. Persegati."

"He's in a meeting and cannot be disturbed. If you leave your number . . ."

"Tell him I've just had a visit from a reporter from *L'Osservatore Romano*."

Silence, then, "*Un momento, per favore!*"

A moment later, Persegati came on the line: "What's all this about? Anna said something about a reporter."

"Does the name Pietro Corelli ring a bell?"

"*Chi?*"

"Corelli," Rachel repeated. "Cultural editor of *L'Osservatore Romano*. Someone tipped him off about the triptych."

"You didn't tell him anything did you?"

"What do you think?"

"*Bene.*" A pause. "I'll look into it."

Rachel flipped the phone shut and sat down in one of the pews facing the high altar. The situation with the triptych was complicated enough without having the whole issue politicized. Pia was still in Bruges researching the Rogier connection, so she could not have leaked the news. Persegati sounded genuinely shocked and had the most to lose if his museum's deal with Apex became public. Leaving Nigel or Donati. Nigel seemed too straightforward somehow, too honorable. Rachel leaned against the back of the pew and closed her eyes, ironically aware that it would look like she was praying. That left Donati.

She sat on, unable to face work on the central panel. When she first embarked on her career as a conservationist she believed in things like beauty, authenticity, integrity. That was before the Baultenheimer Altarpiece, before her marriage.

As a technician, someone wholly concerned with the integrity of the work, she fancied herself above those who sought art more for the snob value of a big name than the quality of the work itself. Now she suspected it was this air of impregnability, a kind of virginal severity so different from the worldliness of Mark's previous girl-friends, that initially attracted him, made him feel as if initiating her into his own world was a kind of cultural deflowering. The thought nauseated her.

Prior to the fiasco with the Baultenheimer, the truth was she had been an idealist, a sort of "art for art's sake" ingenue. Afterwards, she had felt a loss of innocence, a hardening of her ideals, even detachment from the restoration process itself. The real reason she came to Rome was to reforge a connection with her work, a con-nection that used to be passionate, the same passion she saw in Donati.

Thunder rattled overhead and Rachel opened her eyes. The stained glass oriel above the altar had been extinguished by the darkness of the sky outside. By contrast, the sanctuary lamp seemed brighter in the gloom, its flame steady.

She looked at her watch. Eleven-thirty. A white-surpliced Angelo was lighting candles on the altar in readiness for the noon mass. Halfway down the nave, an old woman in a black head scarf mumbled in front of a statue. Rachel saw swollen knuckles and twisted fingers clasping a rosary. Beside her, fanned out, an umbrella glistened as drops of rain slid down to puddle on the floor.

She stood up as Donati walked in through the main doors.

"Hey," he said. Plastered to his head, his hair looked darker, straighter, when wet; raindrops glistening at the clumped ends and in his lashes. In an habitual gesture Rachel recognized, he wiped his cheek on his arm by hunching his shoulder, something he did when both hands were busy on the triptych. "How's the panel coming?"

"Haven't started yet," Rachel replied. "I still need to set up the lights."

"I'll do it."

"Thanks."

Once the lights were plugged in, Rachel turned to face him. Drying now, his hair fell over his forehead. Wanting to reach out and smooth it back so she could see his eyes, she asked, "Where were you this morning?"

"Something came up."

"Such as?"

"It's personal."

81

"What you mean is, it's none of my business?"

"Something like that." He took off his jacket and unwound a scarf from around his neck, draping both on the back of a chair. Slowly, he began to roll up his sleeves.

"Did you contact Pietro Corelli?"

"Not recently."

"So you know him."

"Not well, but we meet at exhibits from time to time, chat, swap art world gossip, that kind of thing. Look, what's this about?"

"He was here this morning asking questions."

Donati paused in the process of unbuttoning one of his cuffs. "And you think I had something to do with it?"

"It seems likely." Outside another rumble of thunder, louder.

"Let me get this straight," Donati said. "You think it was me who tipped Pietro off?"

"Under the heading of 'art-world gossip' perhaps."

"I see." Unlike in Gino's when she tried to goad a reaction out of him, he smiled but this time there was no light in his eyes. "If I wanted to do real damage, I'd go further than dropping a hint. I'd write a bloody press release, stage a press conference on the steps of the church. Picture it, all the major networks, irate parishioners, the works."

"Is that a threat?"

"What do you think?"

Another crash of thunder and out of the corner of her eye, Rachel saw a drop of water gather, plump, then fall onto the stone floor. It was swiftly followed by another, then another, until there was a steady stream. She had already spoken to the monsignor about the leak in the roof, but he had just shrugged. "What can I do?" he said. "There is no money."

"Is this what you want?" Rachel said, flinging her arm around the chapel. It was as if she had suddenly seen it for the first time: the thick layer of soot and dust that coated the altar, the floor, and even the smallest outcropping of stone or statuary; the walls deeply scored with cracks; and the puddle that was rapidly forming at her feet.

She kicked at the jumble of bottles and instruments in danger of being overtaken by the encroaching water then stooped to place a basin beneath the flow. It would be full in less than ten minutes. "Face it," she said. "In five years all our work will have been for nothing. The parish can't even raise enough money to mend the roof for God's sake, let alone protect a solitary work of art."

Just then the bell sang to signal the beginning of Mass. Rachel remembered the woman's hands and the pathetic brightness of the crucifix.

"What does that have to do with it?" Donati said. "So what if the roof leaks? It doesn't alter the fact that the triptych's important to them."

"But they don't even know what they're looking at!" Rachel was angry at herself for becoming emotional. She felt she was arguing with herself as much as with Donati. "In it's present state, it's practically worthless."

"Who the hell are you to judge that?"

"It's my job. *Your* job."

Just then the altar bell rang. Rachel realized she was shaking. She walked over to the gate and watched as a handful of communicants filed forward. Angelo held the gold paten steady as some received the wafer on their tongue, others in their palm, right hand cupped beneath left. It was soon over. Angelo and the priest returned to the altar and began to clean the chalices. When the door to the tabernacle clicked shut and the priest had genuflected, the congregation settled back in the pews to await the final blessing, the dismissal.

Donati had come over to stand beside her. Rachel could feel his breath on her cheek, smell the rain on his clothes. "Look," he said. "It wasn't me who leaked to the press." He touched her shoulder: "I wouldn't betray the project. You."

The pupils of his eyes dilated, black swamping brown, saying something. Rachel didn't know how to respond so she said nothing. The atmosphere in the chapel was brittle as if something had changed between them. She could hear the rain drumming on the roof.

XII

RACHEL FOUND DONATI ALREADY IN THE CHAPEL when she arrived. A paper plate with what looked like marinara sauce and a half-eaten roll rested on one of the chairs, a beer can rolled away as her toe nudged it. Pale and in need of a shave, his eyes were red-rimmed.

"You look like hell."

"*Grazie.*"

"So why the all-nighter?"

Donati gestured towards the central panel. "Dr. Piers, meet Rogier Van der Weyden; Rogier, Dr. Piers."

The transformation was astounding. The previous day the blackened surface revealed only the faintest ghosting of forms, now the central panel was a coherent tableau of color and movement. Except for one figure that had yet to be uncovered, the two main characters were now fully revealed. Christ and Mary.

The triptych was indeed the work of Rogier Van der Weyden. The clue lay in the linear rhythms of the mother's body, rather than in the abstract austerity of the background scene. Although partially obscured by the sprawling body of her Son, Mary's upper torso clearly described a swooning backwards motion with the draperies of her robes falling into long, open arcs around her. It was one of the canons of art history that Rogier had been the first to depict Mary falling into a lifeless faint at the sight of her crucified Son.

Delicate shadings of gray highlighted with light tints of pink, blue and white, indicated Rogier's famous grisaille method, a method he employed to give a feeling of weightlessness and transparency to his figures, which, in turn, gave them an air of vulnerability as if what they witnessed was too painful to support. She turned her attention back to the face.

Where she had expected the traditional medieval serenity and holy stoicism usually reserved for depictions of the Virgin, Rachel found herself looking at an emotion so raw, so utterly devoid of hope she might have been looking at a *Time* magazine photograph of an Iraqi widow.

"I know Rogier is famous for his depiction of emotion," Rachel murmured, "but this is . . ."

"Brutal?" Donati offered.

"Nihilistic. If this had been a painting by Matthias Grunewald, I could understand." She thought of his magnificently graphic crucifixion scene on the central panel of the Isenheim Altarpiece.

"And see here," Donati said. "He depicted Mary as an old woman."

Rachel ran the magnifying glass over the face, tracing the age lines around Mary's eyes and forehead, noting the green and yellow skin tones.

"Unusual," she said. "Maybe this was painted at the end of his life? After all, Michelangelo's Rondanini *Pieta* is radically different from his earlier one."

In the earlier Pieta, the Mother of Christ was portrayed as an exact contemporary of her Son, the sculpture radiating a beauty and serenity that completely overpowered the tragedy of the event. Obviously the work of a brash young man at the height of his career.

The Rondanini was another matter. Michelangelo not only depicted Mary as an old crone, but showed her sagging under the weight of her dead son and her grief. Michelangelo died before it was finished; a fitting epitaph, Rachel always thought, for a man who saw both the best and worst that the Catholic church had to offer. She thought of him on a rickety scaffold far above the Sistine Chapel, suffering unbearable cramps in his shoulders, and losing his eyesight. He labored over it for years, and for what? A cursory Papal blessing and a bag of gold. Perhaps it was a kind of penance. Vasari, his contemporary biographer, said he was wracked with remorse over his profligate youth.

Gently, Rachel drew the sheet back over the triptych. "Something doesn't add up," she said. "I know Rogier became more ascetic in his old age, especially after his son entered the Carthusian monastery, but the emotional tone is too intense, even for him. The technique is the same, the tone is different. It's like this is a Rogier, yet not a Rogier."

An hour later they were seated in an upper story restaurant off the Piazza Campo Dei Fiori opposite the Farnese Palace. Frescoed on the walls, shapely Botticellian nymphs danced with stately steps and linked hands while muscular youths looked on in a delirium of adolescent longing. Most of the tables were occupied and the sound of conversation combined with the dense peopling on the walls created a sense of vibrancy that Rachel found exhilarating after months of comparative solitude. It made her realize how withdrawn she had become, how reluctant to connect with the world around her. She wondered if that had been Donati's intention in inviting her here.

"Not exactly high art," said Donati, seeing the direction of Rachel's gaze.

"I like it," she said. "It's cheery." A far cry from Gino's.

"So, what'll it be?"

Something bland. Since her arrival she had practically lived on bread, coffee and water, anything fancier made her nauseated. At first she dismissed it as the flight, the new job, the trauma of the attack the first night, but, recently, it had become a problem.

While Donati ordered, he and the waiter traded gossip over the latest political scandal. Now shadowed, now revealed, the planes and contours of his jaw-line, his brow, the delicate ridging of his lips, fluctuated in the soft track lighting above his head giving him a look of intense animation as it caught him from unexpected angles. Used to working with him in close proximity, Rachel was more familiar with the stillness of his profile as he bent over the triptych, the sound of his voice as they discussed the panels. This sudden and unexpected manifestation of the wholeness and complexity of his person threw her off, made her wonder what he could see of her from across the table.

With an effort, Rachel brought herself back to what they were saying. Her Italian was patchy, but she caught something about a high ranking official recently arrested for graft. Inveighing against the corruption in the system, she nonetheless caught the irony in Donati's voice.

He professed to believe passionately in his political ideals, but was cynical about them at the same time. He claimed to be an agnostic, yet his hand twitched whenever the bell signaled the consecration, as if he were about to make the sign of the cross. Since confronting him about the media leak he had reverted to a banked-down strictly professional mode, discussing only the project and remaining silent much of the time. Neither of them mentioned the incident. Then today, as they were packing up, Donati asked her if she had plans for the evening.

"No," Rachel admitted. "I was going to look over the first report again to see if there's anything we could have missed. Get an early night." Boring. Pathetic. *Get a life, Rachel.*

"I know a place," he said.

Rachel laid down her fork. She had only been able to eat a little.

"That was only the first course," Donati joked. His own plate had been wiped clean long ago, and he was in the process of reaching for his third roll from the basket in the center of the table. "You're looking thin." This time his voice was serious.

Rachel had to laugh. "You sound like Mark, my ex."

"Mark?" Donati tore off a piece of bread and dipped it in the olive oil puddled on his plate. His movements were casual, relaxed, but his eyes were focused and alert. "Tell me about him," he said. "When did you two meet?"

She met Mark, she told him, at a cocktail party at her museum two years ago. She'd come directly from work on the Baultenheimer in another wing and arrived late. He was standing in the center of the room talking to the head curator. The overhead lights turned his hair to a burnished gold that was echoed richly in links of his wrist-watch and cufflinks. Most of the other guests had already left. He was drinking red wine.

Donati raised his glass. "We men really are bastards."

"Rachel, come and meet Mr. Prescott," the curator said. "He's going to build our new wing for us." She didn't remember much of the conversation, something about the new wing, then a little about her work on the altarpiece. What she did recall was the ease with which Mark steered the flow of conversation. They left the museum together. Mark offered to share a taxi downtown.

Rachel glanced at Donati. He was looking at his glass, stroking his finger up and down the sides, his expression unreadable.

What she didn't tell him was that later, over dinner, Mark said when he first saw her at the door, he had been struck by two things: the austerity of her appearance and her uncertainty. Both, he said, showed in her face—the straight jaw and nose, the sharply defined mouth, the gray eyes that swiveled uneasily about the room. He said he felt he knew her by just looking at the contours and lines, like a building.

Then Mark leaned across the table and took her face in his hands. Her hair was pulled back, revealing a slight widow's peak that drew attention to the whiteness of her forehead. Her lips were bare of lipstick and, unlike the other women in the room, she wore no ornamentation of any kind, not even a ring. The only luxury she allowed herself was perfume. He told her she looked like a nun, but a fragrant one.

She pulled back from him then, embarrassed. She said she didn't usually deck herself out for work and that was where she'd been moments before they met.

"He liked my commitment to the job," Rachel said.

"That's certainly one of your trademarks," Donati murmured.

"Except he thought it was ambition."

"And it isn't."

It took a few moments for Rachel to realize it wasn't a question. She looked up, startled. His awareness intrigued her, troubled her. Her fierce joy in stripping away the accumulated detritus of dirt and varnish, of uncovering, inch by inch, section by section, original pigment and the miracle of form, sprang from a passionate need to recover something blighted, something lost through human neglect and the obscuring overlay of time. If Donati could see that then he might also see the place she kept hidden, a place so private, so intimate, only she knew it existed. For the second time that evening she wondered whether accepting his invitation tonight was a mistake.

"I'm guessing no kids."

"No." She looked at the coffee in her cup, cold with the strip of lemon peel floating on top. She put it down.

Soon after they first met she and Mark became lovers. They had gone back to his apartment after an opera at the Metropolitan. *Madame Butterfly*, or maybe *Aida*.

During their lovemaking Rachel kept hearing the strains of one of the arias fading away in one long, last heartbreaking note.

Afterwards, while Mark slept, she lay awake in the darkness listening to his breathing and marveled at her separateness. When she dressed in the chill milkiness of dawn she felt the secret joy of her private life enveloping her once again. She left a note on his pillow. "Gone to work." It was five-thirty in the morning.

Donati hunched over the table. "So Mark built the new wing to house the Baultenheimer," he said.

"Yes. Not only is the new wing hideously anachronistic with the rest of the museum, but I was assured the Baultenheimer would be returned to Germany after its completion. I learned later that Mark knew it was slated to be housed in his wing all along."

"*Jesu.*"

The scaled-down model of the new wing in the Apex headquarters in New Jersey was perfect in every way, even down to the tiny plastic trees lining its perimeter. When the actual building was completed it looked like the model miraculously blown up to size. "Flawless," Mark kept saying. "Absolutely flawless."

"So you see," she said. "I have no love for Apex either."

They sat on, unmolested by waiters anxious to lock up. Another advantage to being the proprietor's cousin, Rachel supposed.

"What about you?" she asked after a while.

"You mean have I ever been married?"

"I suppose so."

"No. Came close once, but it didn't work out."

"Tell me about your family."

"I have a niece," Donati said. "Several, in fact, but only one here in Rome. Her mother, my sister, is single. I help her out when I can. That morning I was late, I was babysitting. She was sick and my sister couldn't get off work."

"Why didn't you tell me?"

Donati shrugged. "I didn't know you well enough. Anyway, it would seem contrived, the perfect alibi."

"It must be hard for your sister."

"It is."

"Is her father still around?"

"Took off before she was born."

Rachel had only the most tenuous recollection of her own father, more like a longing that would grip her suddenly, than a clearly defined picture. Of course, her mother had shown her photographs, but the glazed smile of the young man holding the bland-eyed baby did not move her. It was like looking at snapshots of somebody else's vacation, happy, remote.

What she did remember were her parents' wedding rings. As a very young child Rachel loved to twist them round and round on their fingers, and when she put her eye close she could see the room reflected within them, perfectly, completely, magically. They were silvery and shiny, only they weren't silver, her mother told her, they were made out of white gold. To Rachel that made them seem even more enchanting. Her father's ring was thicker, plainer, but she could see more of the room in it. When he vanished from her life, so had the rings, along with the little world inside them. Later, she learned he died of cancer when she was three.

Outside, the outline of the Farnese Palace was erased by night; headlights passed, scything the darkness, creating a wedge of light in which, briefly illuminated, rain fell steadily. Inside, many of the tables were empty; waiters moved silently about the floor, replacing cutlery, folding napkins, tucking bills discreetly under plates. Donati signaled to one of them.

"Excuse me a minute," Rachel said, getting up. Throughout the day, a dull, dragging ache in her lower body reminded her she was overdue for her period. Heading for the bathroom in the back of the restaurant, she dreaded it catching her unprepared. Thankfully, there was no sign of it. Rinsing her hands under the faucet afterwards, she wasn't worried. Her monthly cycle was as haphazard and capricious as an adolescent girl's.

Salvatore, Donati's cousin, was making a show of counting his money when she returned. "Watch out for this one," he said, winking at her. Then he grabbed Donati in a bear hug, kissed him twice on each cheek, but not before Rachel saw him tuck Donati's money into his back pocket. "Don't be a stranger," he shouted as they stepped out into the dark, rain-washed street.

Central Panel

XIII

THE NEXT DAY, RACHEL WOKE, conscious that the ache of the day before had become a stabbing pain. She drew up her knees, hugging her pillow. Definitely her period.

She took a couple of Advil, and was just drifting off again when the phone rang. She let it ring a few times, hoping it would stop, then lunged for it, missed, and had to reel it in by its cord.

"Rachel."

"*Mom?*"

Background noise. A loud speaker announcing something, then the words, "Excelsior . . . nine . . . breakfast." Another pause, then: "I'm in Rome shopping for clients."

Much in demand by New York's beau monde, bored with neo-*Bauhaus*, Andy Warhol knockoffs, and the sterility of chrome tubing and glass, Rachel's mother was an interior designer specializing in Napoleonic era neo-Baroque. A look that hadn't been chic since the hey-day of the Du Ponts and the Henry James American nouveaux riches of the nineteenth century, it reveled in heavy gilt furniture, layers of brocade against intricately painted tiles and dark wood, with lots of clocks, figurines, and knickknacks reflected in enormous gold-toned mirrors. To Rachel it looked like a Disney version of Ali Baba's cave, overstuffed, a riot of competing colors, textures and way too many shiny surfaces. Rachel found it decadent, stifling. She loathed the painters from that era, especially David, whose indolent, buxom goddesses reclining on plush sofas made her gag, although she had to admit his technique was accomplished. But her mother made a comfortable living gutting and refurbishing brownstones, giving face-lifts to hotel ballrooms and lobbies. One of her clients had been the actress Faye Dunaway. Others had been a Helmsley hotel and the Plaza.

"See you soon. Don't forget. Nine o'clock at the Excelsior."

Rachel hung up. The sheets had cooled, and she moved her legs around trying to find a warm spot.

If her mother just landed, it would take at least a couple of hours to get to the hotel and settle in. Typical of her not to ask if her unexpected visit was convenient but then she had never been able to imagine herself into Rachel's life. Which made her profession all the more puzzling to Rachel. The ability to see color, texture, light, style in a bare room took imagination. Perhaps Rachel was too near to come into focus, a blur in the foreground against an otherwise clear horizon.

There was another snag. She had promised Donati she would meet him at the church at nine to continue work on the central panel. They had stood outside

Salvatore's for some time discussing it: if Mary was in a swoon, then someone must be holding her up. John, the beloved disciple.

Rachel drew the covers over her head and scrunched into a tight ball. Her favorite position since she was little.

Donati. He insisted on accompanying her back to her apartment, but refused to come in. She apologized for believing he was the one who talked to the media, thanked him for dinner.

"*Prego*," he said. Unprotected by the courtyard, the wind staggered into them, lashing Rachel's hair across her face, flinging a ground floor shutter against a wall with sullen monotony. Donati reached out and hooked a strand of hair back over Rachel's ear, his fingertips briefly brushing her cheek. "*A domani*," he said. Till tomorrow.

Rachel wondered how long her mother planned to stay. Please God not more than a few days. The emotions she awoke, emotions that left Rachel edgy, scrambled, obscurely guilt-ridden were more than she could bear right now.

Another cramp. Rachel gave up being able to go back to sleep. She decided to run a bath.

Rachel arrived at the Excelsior at eight-forty-five. "Evelyn Piers," she told the receptionist on the desk. Her mother had reverted to Rachel's father's name after divorcing her second husband.

"Who shall I say is here?" the man asked.

"Her daughter."

"*Un momento, per favore*." He picked up the phone

and after a short conversation said, "She say to go up, *Signorina. Numero* five-zero-five."

"*Grazie.*"

Rachel rode up in the elevator. A woman and two children got in on the third floor. "Going up," Rachel said. "Sorry." The woman looked annoyed and ushered the children out again.

Room 505 was a left out of the elevator, then hard right. A maid in a black dress and white apron and cap rattled by with a trolley piled with breakfast trays. Rachel knocked.

"Just leave it by the door," her mother called.

"It's me."

The door opened.

"I thought it was the maid," her mother said. "I ordered the *New York Times* fifteen minutes ago."

"Hi, Mom," Rachel said, kissing her cheek.

Petite, with regular features and auburn hair, now dyed, Evelyn Piers was sixty-five but looked fifty.

"Don't just stand there. Come in for goodness sake."

Rachel followed her into the room.

Mrs. Piers picked up a pair of reading glasses and squinted at an open leather folder.

"I was just looking at the menu," she said. "I thought we'd order up."

"Fine." Rachel took off her coat and sank down in one of the armchairs by the fire. A huge four-poster hung with machine-woven tapestries was dwarfed by the cavernous room. Embossed medallions depicting heads of various Roman emperors covered the ceiling, cunningly executed in faded gold and enamel to give the effect of antiquity. Volcanic logs crackled under an

100

impressively gilded marble fireplace giving off a surprising amount of heat.

"Waffles or pancakes?" her mother asked, hand over the receiver.

"Whatever." Rachel put her feet up on the coffee table to ease the pain in her gut.

"Both," Mrs. Piers said into the phone, "and coffee. For two. Regular. And make sure it's hot."

Rachel rested her head against the chair. On some level she found her mother's ability to plow through life admirable, even heroic. Considering the loss of two husbands under tragic circumstances Rachel recognized it as a refusal to give up, a doggedness born of an instinct to survive. It had taken a long time to see this, let alone accept it. When she was younger her mother turned her into an emotional hemophiliac, the slightest nick causing her to gush rage, resentment and a ravening need for approval. Leaving for college helped but it had taken her twenties for her to let go of her incomprehension, the emptiness she felt inside. Now she felt her own identity distinct from rather than intrinsic to her mother's. A marriage counselor she and Mark visited a few times said her increasing detachment was a good thing. Rachel wasn't so sure. Maybe it was a sign she had given up.

"Thank you." Evelyn Piers put the phone down and came to stand in front of Rachel. "Let me have a look at you. Mmm." She tilted her head to one side, considering. "I expect you're working too hard. As usual."

"I love you too," Rachel returned, too quietly to be heard.

"So," her mother said, sitting opposite. "What have you been up to? Met any interesting people?"

"I've been busy."

"Mmm," her mother said again. A knock on the door.

While room service brought in breakfast, Rachel went into the bathroom and took more Advil. The pain, if anything, was worse.

"I have to make a call," she said when she came out.

"The food's getting cold."

"It won't take long. You go ahead."

Rachel perched on the edge of the bed and punched in Donati's cell phone number.

"What you want?"

"It's Dr. Piers—Rachel." Sometimes Donati left his phone in the chapel and Angelo picked it up.

"Rachel, Rachel—" She could hear him repeating her name over and over, each time growing fainter.

"Angelo, put the phone back to your ear." She heard a crash as he dropped it, then hoarse breathing.

"Is Donati there?"

"Hey, it's me. What's up?"

"Listen," she said. "I can't make it in this morning. Something's come up. Can you meet me later tonight in the chapel?"

"Sure." A pause. "Is everything all right?"

"Fine," she replied. "Everything's fine. See you tonight."

"Who's Donati?" her mother asked when Rachel hung up.

"The pigment analysis expert I work with." Rachel sat opposite and found herself staring at an enormous plate of ham, eggs, pancakes and a side serving of waffles. She would much rather have had the fruit plate her

102

mother ordered for herself. "How long will you be here?" she asked, prodding the meat with her fork. It was underdone and flopped over like a salacious pink tongue. So much for the Excelsior's boast that it provided American tourists with a slice of home. Obviously their chef had not yet mastered the art of cooking a trucker's breakfast. She gave up and took a sip of tomato juice.

"What day is it?" her mother asked. "I've lost track."

"Friday."

"Through the weekend, then. Tuesday I fly to Paris. There's a fabric show and a couple of chateau auctions I need to catch." She looked at Rachel over the top of her coffee cup, her expression unreadable.

"What?" Rachel asked when she didn't speak.

"I ran into Mark the other day at the Pierre."

Rachel coughed. A sharp corner of waffle had gone down the wrong way. She sipped more juice to help it down, aware that her mother was waiting for her to say something. When she didn't she said, "He looked well. He said . . ."

"Mother," Rachel said putting her fork down, careful not to clatter it. "I'm really not interested in how Mark is or what he said or who his clients are or what kind of car he's driving, or who he's seeing now or anything about him. It's over. All right?" She reached round the flowers on the tray and poured herself a cup of coffee. "If that's what you've really come to Rome to talk about then you're going to be disappointed."

Evelyn Piers said nothing and Rachel rode the ensuing silence with relative calm. A bubble detached itself from the stem of one of the roses in the bud vase on her tray and wavered to the surface. She touched the frond of baby's breath making the tiny flowers shiver on their spiky stems. That was another thing she was learning, that she wasn't the only one who carried the burden of keeping their relationship going. Something else the marriage counselor taught her.

She pushed her plate away. The congealing food was beginning to make her ill.

"I thought you were hungry?"

"I never said that."

Her mother patted her lips with her napkin, then folded it into a neat, white square, sweeping thumb and forefinger down the edges until they were exactly aligned. "I don't understand you, Rachel. You don't eat, you certainly don't communicate. You go rushing off to Rome to restore some painting like you wanted to escape. If you needed a break you could have gone to the cabin."

Summers spent at her stepfather's cabin by the lake, shrieking with delicious terror as he disappeared under water to catch her suddenly round the legs, lifting her bodily out of the water. She remembered the hardness of his chest against her thighs, the slithery caress of the water as it ran down her shoulders over childishly pointed breasts. Then the sky reeling and the shock of cold as he tossed her backwards. After the divorce the property had passed to her mother as part of the settlement. Rachel hadn't been there in over twenty years.

She didn't need a temporary break in a routine she would pick up again when she returned, she needed to slough off an old skin that had become dry, constricting. Somehow she had to find a way to emerge whole. How could she explain that to her mother when she barely understood it herself?

She glanced at her watch. "I've got to go. Thanks for breakfast."

"I thought you weren't meeting what's-his-name till this evening."

"There are things I have to do." Rachel put on her coat and walked to the door. "I'll call tomorrow. Maybe we can do something together?"

In the large room, Evelyn Piers suddenly looked fragile and doll-like.

Relenting, Rachel walked back, bent to kiss her. "Bye, Mom."

XIV

THE SKY, CONCRETE, HEAVY LIKE IT MIGHT SNOW, made her shiver and settle farther back in the seat of the cab. A tableau of faces, bodies, vehicles, spooled by. A Fellini film, dream-like but acutely detailed: a baby's fist waving from a stroller; a woman in high heels and full-length fur standing at a newspaper stand; an old man in cloth cap and checkered muffler talking to himself with eloquent, fluttering hand-motions; blood-red geraniums in cracked terra-cotta pots spotting balconies with violent color; a white cloth snapping over a railing sending a flurry of pigeons into the air, flapping and wheeling before settling back in the same spot.

The cab stopped and it was some moments before Rachel realized the driver was saying something. His tone was patient, but his eyes in the rear-view mirror said *Crazy foreigners.*

She paid him and got out, her legs rubbery, her head a balloon bobbing on a string above her body.

106

Rachel intended to change and go straight to the church. If she hurried she would catch Donati before he went to lunch, but by the time she climbed the stairs and opened the door she knew she had to lie down. She kicked her shoes off, crawled under the covers fully clothed and rested her head against the crook of her arm. The cashmere of her sweater felt soft, comforting, but not warm enough, even the dim light hurt her eyes, and from outside the sound of traffic came to her like a low roar.

It was early evening when Rachel woke. She stumbled to the bathroom, clicked on the light, splashed water on her face, then looked in the mirror. Dark, feverish eyes surrounded by chalk-white skin. It didn't look anything like her. But the pain was the same. She gripped the edge of the sink, bending forward. No. It was worse.

Opening the bathroom cabinet, she rummaged around for painkillers: razor blades, hand lotion, a couple Band-Aids, travel-size mouthwash, a comb. She upset a bottle of talcum powder and it spurted over her sleeve. No Advil. She must have taken the last of it at the hotel.

Holding onto the wall, she made her way back to the living room, grabbed her purse and without even bothering to pick up her coat, left the apartment. Somehow she had to find a pharmacy. She tried to think of the sign for drug store. A staff and serpent? She knew the sign was illuminated and stuck out sideways over the street so it was easy to see, especially at night. Outside the gate, Rachel looked first left, then right, wondering which way to go.

A blue cross. She must find one.

How long she wandered the streets, she didn't know, but by the time she found herself in front of the church, it had been dark for several hours. Pushing with all her strength, she opened the door, and using the pillars for support, made her way towards the chapel. Perhaps Donati was working late.

Someone had lit a votive candle on the altar and shadows writhed on the walls and panels of the triptych. Rachel felt her forehead. It burned and the floor beneath her was strangely wet. She made a mental note to tell the monsignor that the roof was leaking again.

It was then that she became aware of someone calling her name.

Her back hurt. She spread her arms, hands contacting tiles. She was lying down. Funny, she didn't remember doing that.

Her skirt was pushed up and her thighs felt sticky. She was cold, colder than she'd ever been before and there was a stabbing between her legs. Her hands moved to her face and she tasted salt.

"*Madonna*!"

There it was again. The house was silent, watchful, the trees black against the sky and very still. No breeze. It was growing dark and the moon was rising, rising above the walls, above the tangle of branches, above the clouds, rising above everything that hemmed her in and oppressed her, and as it rode the sky it seemed to catch her up in its light.

Rachel opened her eyes and saw Angelo's face. Then another.

"We have to get you to a hospital," a voice said.

Someone was lifting her. Gray forms drifted past like trees in the mist. Somewhere in the distance a red eye was watching, and Rachel heard the insistent thump, thump of a heartbeat close to her ear.

A rush of cold air on her face, then someone tucking something about her. So that's where she was. Lying in the snow behind her mother's Long Island house on a winter afternoon.

"Rachel, you have to stay awake."

She opened her eyes. How did Donati get there?

A sharp prick in her arm. She must be dreaming. It wasn't Donati at all, but her best friend, Maggie; they were lying on a carpet of pine needles in the woods. This was their secret place, their refuge. They had become friends in third grade when Rachel realized that Maggie, like her, was always running from something.

Maggie, red curls, a constellation of freckles across the bridge of her nose, the youngest of ten, was always being tormented by someone—anyone. Either one of her brothers, or her Mom trying to get her to do chores around the house. "*Maargreet Meeery!*" she would yell from the back stoop. They used to hear her voice from the woods and giggle. "I hate that name," Maggie said.

"It's not so bad. It's just the way she says it." And Rachel would imitate the Irish pronunciation, sending them off into fits again.

Now someone was shaking her. One of Maggie's brothers; Billy, most likely. He was twelve and always spying on them.

"Go away," Rachel said.

"Can't this thing go any faster?"

Rachel wondered why Billy was speaking Italian.

"It's all right, *signore*," a woman said. "Not far now."

It was then she realized that she was in an ambulance screaming through the streets of Rome.

Rachel lay inert in the hospital bed, riding the waves of pain that surged through her lower body. She heard Donati talking with someone outside the room, then the sudden clatter of a metal dish being dropped. Another spasm began, surreptitiously, then with increasing force. She closed her eyes and dug her nails deeper into the coverlet. They had told her to expect afterbirth pains.

Afterbirth.

The word mocked her. There had been no slippery rush of life, no bleating cry, no blind mouth mumbling at her breast. There had been nothing but a bloody mess that glistened darkly under the fluorescent lights and filled the air with the sickly odor of failure. She saw one of the nurses cover a basin with a white cloth and put it on a steel trolley by the door as casually as bread left to rise. A corner of the napkin had fallen into the bowl and a bloom of red began to grow on the white.

She lay there staring at it while they cleaned her up. They thought she hadn't noticed.

The face of Mary in the triptych came to her then. A mother's face, twisting with anguish as it looked down at the body of her child, knowing it for the body she had delivered into the filthy straw, the body she had bathed and suckled, the body she had caught in her arms as it tottered its first steps towards her, crowing in triumph. It was the face of a woman who knows she is holding her child for the last time.

The pain began to ebb away, a brief respite before gathering strength for the next assault. Warily, Rachel relaxed her grip. The door opened, then closed. She heard footsteps moving softly across the floor.

For a moment, Rachel thought it was her mother, then she saw Donati. By the time they got to the hospital she was slipping in and out of consciousness, but each time she opened her eyes, Donati was there. When they tried to make him leave the operating room, he responded with such fury that the doctor just shrugged and tossed him a white gown. "Put this on," he said. "And scrub up."

"Angelo found you," Donati said. He was sitting on the edge of her bed, his body twisted towards her. "He goes to the chapel every night to talk to the triptych.

"He tried to revive you. When that failed, he called me. I could hardly make sense of him at first. He kept babbling something about the Mother coming down from the painting. I found you lying on the floor." He took Rachel's hand. "You lost a lot of blood."

"How far along?" Rachel whispered.

"Twelve weeks."

She turned her face away. So it had been there all along, flickering in the dark. Now the flame had guttered and gone out. Tears gathered, began to trickle out the corners of her eyes, wetting the pillow.

"Don't leave me," she whispered. "Please. Not tonight."

"I won't," he said.

XV

ONE OF THE FLUORESCENT TUBES above Rachel's head flickered and chirred as if a moth were caught inside, waking her. A plastic pouch on an IV stand dripped clear liquid into a vein through a tube taped to the top of her left hand. Another, hooked up to a chrome monitor and attached to the artery in her wrist, fed something red into her. She had no recollection of them being put in.

The top of Donati's head lay on the bed, his cheek resting on folded arms. Close up she could see his hair waved in places, smelled resiny as if it had picked up a scent from the lab. He stirred but continued to sleep, his breathing regular, barely audible.

He had kept vigil all night, rarely speaking, holding a cup to her lips when she was thirsty, helping her settle back on the pillows. Sometimes Rachel dozed, sometimes lay staring at the ceiling, grateful for his silence, his presence.

Sometime between true darkness and the first hint of dawn she told him about her stepfather, the rape, abortion, her mother, omitting nothing. As she spoke, light began to limn the umbrella pines on the Janiculum hill, gradually teasing green from black until they stood in full relief.

"Sleep now," he said when she was done.

Rachel could hear doors opening and shutting, the trundle of trolleys, running water, doctors being paged, but felt exempted, motionless, like the center of a pinwheel amidst a blur of movement.

And like a wheel, her life had come full circle. Twelve weeks. The fetus had fingers, toes, gender, was able to move about, float freely in the space her body made. And she had not known, had not even guessed. It didn't matter the baby was Mark's, conceived in a moment of lust, loneliness and stupidity, instantly regretted. What mattered was what came after, the first tentative seeding, the moist concavity of a receptive womb, budding, growth.

The first time it happened her ignorance was a shield, a blessed amnesia, screening her from the logic of her violation, of a childhood taken and discarded before she was ready to relinquish it.

Now her ignorance felt like sin, a sword that pierced her heart.

For her, life could be understood only by its ending, all knowledge retrospective, tinged with shame and remorse, a punishment for harboring some taint, some virus that entered her the moment her stepfather forced her legs apart.

A yearning gripped her, terrible and all-consuming, filling the room until she felt awash with agony. She clutched at the covers, legs writhing.

Donati lifted his head, his cheek patterned where it had lain on his arms, his eyes unfocused, then clearing

113

when he saw Rachel. He reached along the side of the bed and pressed a buzzer.

A nurse appeared almost at once.

"My friend's in pain," he said. "She needs something. *Presto*!"

The woman glanced at Rachel's chart, took her pulse, made a clicking sound in her throat, then left. She came back a few moments later, stuck a syringe into an opening in the IV and depressed the plunger.

"There," she said. "You should be more comfortable now."

"*Grazie*." Rachel wanted to ask if there was a drug that could numb the other pain, the one that never went away.

She reached for Donati's hand. "Thank you," she meant to say, but the words wouldn't come.

In answer, she felt the pressure of his fingers.

She lay there, the silence stretching out, an infinite distance, then curving back on itself until they were enclosed. A stillness she had felt when they worked together in the chapel enveloped her, the stillness of the church, sanctuary of the wounded and betrayed, the stillness of the shadowy figures emerging from the triptych after centuries of patient waiting, Donati's stillness.

The door opened and a male orderly backed in with a tray. He set it down on a sidetable and swiveled it across the bed so it would be within reach. "Breakfast," he said.

"When can I go home?" Rachel asked.

"You'll have to ask the doctor when she comes in this afternoon," the nurse said. "Dr. Fabiola."

Rachel glanced at the tray. "Can you bring some coffee?" *Home*. Odd she phrased it that way.

114

"Sorry. Restricted diet. You'll have to take that up with the doctor."

"At least some for my friend," Rachel said.

The man glanced at Donati then back to Rachel. "I'll see what I can do."

Rachel poked at a pastry on her plate, sticky, blobbed with yellow jam. "I'll trade you this for your coffee," she said.

"Uh, uh," Donati said. "You should eat something."

"You sound like one of them" Rachel said. "Besides, yellow's not my color."

"*Mulo!*"

"What did you say?"

"Mule. I called you a mule."

The nurse came back with a cup. "If you want more," he said to Donati, "the cafeteria's on the first floor."

"*Grazie.*" The nurse looked disapproving when Donati handed Rachel the cup but made no comment. He tucked in the covers at the foot of the bed and left.

"Here," Rachel said, after taking a sip. "Have some."

He was bent forward in the chair, elbows on knees, hair mussed, shirt creased and partially untucked as he balanced the cup in his hands. It was how he'd look in the morning, Rachel thought, before he assumed the air of competency. This was his secret self, the side only his family and closest friends saw. He looked younger, more essentially himself, than she had ever seen him.

She, on the other hand, must look like hell. Involuntarily, she raised a hand to her face, felt where her hair was straggly and matted, her lips dry.

"You look fine," Donati said. He returned the cup, watched her drink. "Listen," he said at last. "You said your mother was in Rome. I think I should call her, let her know what's happened."

"No," Rachel said.

"She'd want to know."

Rachel remembered the night her mother walked in on her in the bathroom. It was the week after Thanksgiving, almost five months after the rape. Her stepfather was away on a business trip. He hadn't touched her since.

Rachel had just gotten out of the shower and was reaching for a towel when the door opened. Bent over at an angle, the rounding of her belly was perfectly silhouetted against the light. Taking the towel, Rachel wrapped it around her, never once raising her eyes to her mother's face. Only the goose bumps rising on her arms from the sudden rush of cold air told her the door had shut. Rachel dried herself, then anointed her body with as much of her mother's talcum powder, lotion and scented oil she could find. She walked down the stairs to where her mother was waiting in the living room in a haze of lavender and jasmine.

Her mother had kept Rachel up until four in the morning, alternately threatening and cajoling for the name of the father. "Him," Rachel kept saying, pointing to the framed photograph on the mantle. "It was him." In the end, it had been the paternity blood-test that convinced her.

"Are they still married? Your mother and stepfather, I mean."

"My mother filed for divorce as soon as she found out I was pregnant."

"She didn't press charges?"

Rachel shook her head. "Didn't want the scandal. Plus, she could ask for whatever she liked in the settlement." The cabin by the lake. "Blackmailed him, in a way."

"Did she love him?"

Rachel hadn't thought about it. "Yes," she said after a pause. "I think she did, after a fashion. She never remarried, so maybe that means something."

"You blame your mother for the rape?" No hesitation, no special emphasis on the word.

"Maybe. But I blame her for the abortion more. Getting rid of it—*her* grandchild—was final proof she would do anything to preserve appearances, even if it meant sacrificing me. Up till then, I suppose I cherished the hope that one day I could make her love me, or if not that, at least love her security less. After the abortion . . ." Rachel shrugged. "I gave up."

"Maybe she was afraid?"

"She was my mother." Rachel put the cup on the tray, the coffee suddenly bitter.

"Rachel," Donati said, his voice quiet. "She still needs to be told."

XVI

THE BLOSSOMS NODDED AS HER MOTHER UNWRAPPED THEM from the cellophane, the stems dotted with green scars where the thorns had been.

"Do you have anything I can put them in?" her mother asked.

"Try the water jug," Rachel said. "There's a sink through there."

She came back from the bathroom, put the flowers on a side table next to the bed and sat down again. Neither spoke. Rachel too weary, Donati's absence a sudden bewildering ache. He had shown her mother in, then left, saying he'd be back in an hour.

Time rewound, going back to the same scene—a hospital bed, roses, her mother. All her life she had acquiesced to the pretense that everything was fine so long as you didn't talk about it, so long as you got on with things, whatever that meant. Even as a child she knew her mother, not her, was the fragile one, the one who needed to be shielded from the truth: When her second grade teacher bullied her, Rachel didn't tell; when she fell off her bike and tore up her knees she wore pants until they healed; when her best friend dumped her she said nothing. By the time she was fourteen, the habit was ingrained.

"Are you in pain?" her mother asked.

"Not any more." The question surprised her. "They gave me something."

"I'm glad." Her mother smoothed the sheet folded over Rachel's chest, moved the water jug on the table, fussed with the flowers, her face hidden.

"Mother," Rachel said, reaching out to still her restlessness. "I'm OK. Really."

"It's not that. . . ." Her mother lifted her head, eyes brimming.

"Please don't."

She opened her purse and dug around inside, her movements jerky, almost angry.

"Here." Rachel angled a box of tissues from her bedside table towards her, was relieved when her mother blew her nose, dabbed her eyes, then tucked the tissue into her sleeve, straightening in the chair.

"I'm sorry," Evelyn Piers said. Her voice quavered, a wire strung too tight.

"For what?"

"For everything." The tears started again. "You don't know what it was like, how much of a struggle it was, paying the bills, working, night school, then you following me around the house saying, look at this, look at that, when all I wanted was peace and quiet. I'd have given anything for five minutes alone in those days.

"Then when you were older, your silences, the way you looked at me, judge, jury, executioner, like I was the worst mother in the world." There was a fierceness in her now, her body quivered with it. "But I wasn't. I knew I wasn't."

She looked past Rachel's head as if watching something private, meant only for her, breathing heavily as if speaking had left her winded. "In a way, I knew it then, when it happened. I just didn't seem to be able to stop myself." Her eyes swiveled to Rachel, focusing. "I guess I was more concerned with finding a way out of the problem, getting him out of my life, *your* life, making us safe. I think if I'd thought about it then I would have gone mad. It wasn't until later, when you were in college, that I began to realize how much you must have suffered. But by then I couldn't seem to find the words."

The cracks on the ceiling wavered, reformed, changed from continents to gridlines, faces, then back to continents. A raven cawed in the trees behind the hospital, brakes squealed on the main road running along the Tiber, nearby a truck upended a dumpster full of broken glass, all came successively, discretely, though Rachel knew them to be simultaneous.

"Rachel."

Stirring within her, almost without volition, the first quavering of compassion for the mother who had not spoken her name with tenderness since before the rape.

Hesitantly, almost shyly, Rachel reached out her hand, touched her mother's cheek.

"Thank you for the roses," she said. "They're beautiful."

120

Side Panel
TWO

XVII

"I DON'T SEE WHY NOT," the doctor said in answer to Rachel's question whether she could go today *per favore*. "You're healing nicely, no bleeding to worry about, temperature normal and your friend said you had somewhere to stay while you recuperate." Dr. Lucia Fabiola drew the sheet down over Rachel's legs. "You can sit up now," she said.

"Thanks," said Rachel, her relief profound when Dr. Fabiola turned out to be a woman her own age, ears flashing multiple silver studs, hair razored short and funky. "Does that mean these can come out?" The IVs pulled painfully, hampering her movements. Humiliating to have to ring for a nurse every time she wanted to go to the bathroom.

"*Si.*" Dr. Fabiola disconnected the tubes, removed the tape then slid the needles out with practiced ease. "You lost a lot of blood so you're going to be pretty wiped out for a month or two. I want to see you again at the end of the week. Come to the outpatient clinic here and ask for me." She scribbled something on a piece of paper and handed it to Rachel. "This is a prescription for painkillers. Take only as needed and not more than three a day. You may experience some grogginess and I'd avoid alcohol, it'll make it worse. If you start bleeding again come see me right away." Her manner was breezy yet assured, her hands, when she had examined Rachel, gentle. "*Ciao!*" she said walking out the door.

Rachel slowly swung her legs off the bed and began to dress. When her mother was visiting the day before, Donati had gone to her apartment and gathered together some things she might need. He'd remembered underwear, moisturizer, toothbrush, perfume, robe, but forgot to bring a book or her laptop.

Her watch said five-fifty-three. Donati said he'd be back at six. He'd gone to visit his mother and sister. A Sunday thing, apparently. Rachel tried not to feel forlorn when he left. She'd spent the morning fiddling with the dial on the radio, surfing through European techno pop, Vivaldi, Pavarotti, hysterical commentary of a soccer match, ending up with a sermon given by the Pope. Finally, she turned it off, switched on the TV bolted to a bracket in the corner of the room and watched Sunday Mass at St. Peter's Basilica on the hospital channel, marveling anew at Bernini's stupendous spiral columns holding up the ornate Baroque canopy covering the high altar.

"What do you think you're doing?" Donati said, coming through the door. Six-fifteen.

Rachel was perched on the edge of the bed slipping on her shoes. "They discharged me."

She put a hand on his shoulder to steady herself as she stood up, her fingers dimpling the leather of his jacket. "I'm feeling better." She swung her overnight bag off the bed and would have staggered if Donati hadn't grabbed it from her.

"I can see that."

They got into an elevator. A man tried to step in between them. "Get the next one," Donati said, hitting the lobby button. A fleeting impression of shock on the man's face, then the doors closed.

The floors were counting down.

Four. Two.

Rachel watched them, acutely aware of Donati's nearness in so small a space. In the hospital room their intimacy seemed natural, unforced, an unimpeded flow. Now they were returning to the outside world, Rachel suddenly felt shaky.

Lobby.

The elevator stopped, rose minutely, then settled. Donati held the *Door Shut* button down. "Ready?" he asked.

"I think so," Rachel replied.

"*Bene.*" He let the doors open and they stepped out.

The cab drew up outside a sand-colored building. They hadn't crossed over the Tiber on the Ponte Emanuele but continued straight on the Lungotevere turning right at the Ponte Sisto and winding through narrow side-alleys and streets of the Trastevere district. Rachel climbed out. The building rose in front of her several stories high, a row of buzzers alongside a glass door showed that it was a block of apartments. One of the names was Donati.

She sat down on the steps, already exhausted. Donati was paying the driver.

"*Grazie.*" The cab drove off. He looked down at her, his face concerned. "Come on. It's cold out here." He held out his hand to lift her to her feet.

"I'm not going anywhere until you tell me why we're not at my apartment."

For the first time Donati looked uncertain, even nervous. "The only way they'd release you was if I could vouch you'd be taken care of for at least two weeks."

"Why didn't you tell me?"

"I knew you'd say no."

"You got that right." Rachel reviewed her options. She could walk back to her own place, but it was cold and she was already worn out by the cab drive, her brief foray into normal life. Staying the night in his apartment made her uncomfortable, the situation between them too new, too unknown. She'd have to call a cab later. For now, she needed to sit down somewhere warm.

Donati was unlocking the door with a key. "Relax," he said. "This is where my mother lives."

Backlit by a light coming from an open door in the narrow hallway, a woman opened the door.

"Mama," Donati said, kissing her on both cheeks, "this is Dr. Piers."

Rachel had built up a mental picture of someone like the women she saw going to market on the street, bulky, stolid in black cardigan, headscarf, quite different from the tiny bird-like woman she now saw before her.

"Pleased to meet you, Signora," Rachel said in Italian. "Call me Rachel, *per favore.*"

"I am so sorry about your baby," the woman said. Her brittle, seemingly fragile hand gave a firm answering pressure. "My home is your own. You must come and sit down, have a little dinner, no?" In the light from the hallway, his mother's eyes appeared paler than Donati's, almost golden.

"*Grazie.*"

Signora Donati led the way into a sitting room, told Rachel to make herself comfortable. A clock on the mantle whirred and began to tell the hour. Through the glass dome, Rachel saw wheels turning, meshing, revolving around their axes, coming together, then moving away, but always touching. The last chime ended with two tiny pings, a fingernail tapping against crystal, then nothing but a low, rhythmic tick. It was seven o'clock.

She reluctantly agreed to stay. "But tomorrow I go back to my own place," she said when Signora Donati left the room saying she had to check on something in the kitchen.

"Whatever." Donati threw himself onto the couch, put his feet up and looked at her from across the room.

"What?" Rachel said, after a few moments.

"You look pale," he said.

"Stop fussing," Rachel said.

"*Si, Signora,*" he said, getting up. "Stay put. I'll be back in a minute."

Rachel heard him talking to his mother somewhere in the back of the apartment, rapid Italian interspersed with the sound of pots and pans, the chink of cutlery. Rachel leaned back and closed her eyes. The sounds were more personal, more intimate than those in the hospital. In the early years of her mother's marriage to her stepfather, she used to sit at the kitchen table, covertly watching her stepfather catch her mother round the waist, nuzzle her neck, warmth spreading from Rachel's stomach up through her chest, basking in her mother's happiness, her unexpected girlishness.

Abruptly, she stood up and went in search of the kitchen.

Donati was standing at the sink with his back to her, draining pasta into a colander, steam billowing in clouds as he tossed the contents, then tipped them into a bowl. "Hey," he said.

"Can I do anything?" Rachel said in English. "I feel like a fifth wheel."

"That's exactly what you're not," Donati said, pouring olive oil over the pasta and setting the bowl on the table.

"Here," Signora Donati said. "Would you taste this for me?" She was standing at the stove stirring a large pot that bubbled vigorously, splattering the stove top. She turned down the heat. "Tell me if it needs more salt." Signora Donati cupped her hand under the spoon and held it out to Rachel who blew on it, then put her lips gingerly against the rim.

"*Nessuno*," Rachel replied, shaking her head.

"*Bene*," said Signora Donati. "Please to be seated."

Rachel sat down at a small, round table that stood against the wall behind the door. A cone-shaped ceiling lamp hung low over the center of the table, shining directly onto a bowl filled with the roses Rachel brought with her from the hospital. Spreading in the heat, the petals were beginning to fall now, revealing stamens tipped with yellow dust at the center.

Her mother visited the hospital that morning, told her, apologetically, that she'd received a call from a buyer in Milan who wanted to meet with her, that she would have to fly straight from Milan to Paris.

"Go," Rachel said. "I'm fine now. Really."

"Are you sure?" Evelyn Piers's face puckered with indecision, guilt.

"I'm sure."

"I'll call when I get to Paris," her mother said. "Promise."

After dinner Signora Donati rose to clear the table.

"Let me help," said Rachel. Donati raised an eyebrow but didn't say anything. Sitting with his elbows on the table, he was idly rolling bread into pellets then lining them up in rows on his plate. Her hip accidentally brushed his arm as she carried the dishes to the sink.

Stacking them, she squeezed in detergent, watching it foam up, conscious of Donati's eyes on her, wanting to touch him, feel his hands moving over her back, his breath on her neck. When the sink was full she lifted a plate and swirled a brush over its surface, scrubbing at the spots where the food had dried and hardened. Signora Donati was standing beside her with a dishtowel, her hands ready. Rachel rinsed the plate and handed it to her. Briefly their fingers touched, Rachel's slick with grease and already beginning to redden in the hot water, Signora Donati's cool, dry. Both smiled, a brief acknowledgment between two women engaged in a domestic chore. Donati came from the table and took the dried plates from his mother, stacking them in a cupboard on a top shelf.

Again, Rachel plunged her hands into the water, reluctant to break the rhythm the three of them had unexpectedly fallen into.

"Your mother is a widow?" Signora Donati said, suddenly.

"She remarried. My father died when I was three." Rachel felt around in the water for the last of the knives.

"I'm sorry."

Rachel shrugged. "I barely remember him." Breaking down into filmy rings, the soap scattered as she withdrew a knife, rinsed it, then passed it on.

Dried, Donati placed it in a drawer, knives, forks, spoons, all their own separate compartments, neatly stacked one on top of the other. Her own apartment in Manhattan was outwardly clean and tidy, the hidden places in chaos; cupboards, drawers, closets, all containing a jumble of the useful and the useless, the broken and the whole, things she couldn't bring herself to throw away.

She had just started on the glasses when she heard a phone ring in one of the rooms off the hallway.

Signora Donati wiped her hands on her apron. "I expect that's Father about the parish bazaar." She left the kitchen, then, "*Pronto?*"

Her fingers closing around the last glass, Rachel held it up to the light to check for smudges, a soapy membrane filmed the top like Saran Wrap, refracting blues and yellows from the water swimming on its surface.

"I'll take that," Donati said, holding the dishtowel his mother had discarded.

She rinsed the glass under the tap and held it out to him, her gesture identical to the way they exchanged swabs, brushes, cleaning fluid without taking their eyes off the triptych. When he reached for the glass, she held onto it, pulling it back towards her. He glanced at her, surprised.

"Touch me," she said.

XVIII

A WEEK AFTER LEAVING THE HOSPITAL, Rachel moved back to her apartment. During her stay she learned that Donati's mother was a widow, his father having died six years before. Signora Donati told her one morning as matter-of-factly as if speaking of the weather. Now anxious to resume her normal routine, she told Signora Donati she had imposed on her kindness long enough. Neither Donati nor his mother said anything but Signora Donati told her she must come for dinner one of these nights.

"*Grazie*," Rachel said. "*Grazie mille.*"

Donati borrowed a friend's car and drove her over the Tiber and back into the city proper. "She's like that," Donati said. "Takes everything in her stride. Even my sister's situation. She's raised so many kids nothing surprises her any more." He flicked on the indicator, crunching the gears as he turned a corner. "And then there's her faith."

His profile was calm, concentrated, eyes flicking from mirror to road and back again, but Rachel sensed a tension in him that hadn't been there before. The gears ground again as the car gathered speed.

"Rachel?"

"Huh, uh."

"I've been meaning to tell you something."

"You accidentally set fire to the lab with one of your cigarettes and destroyed all our samples."

He glanced at her. "My mother had a Mass said for your baby. I thought you should know."

The outline of the trees lining the river suddenly looked so sharp they appeared to be cut out of paper. Carefully, Rachel repeated the word to herself.

Baby.

When a soul fled to God, it went as a naked newborn child, or so the medievals believed, emerging from the mouth of the deceased like a second birth. Her colleagues laughed at her for her delight in what they termed "medieval primitivism," those deathbed scenes with naked infants hovering overhead. Like a storybook ending it was not something Rachel believed so much as wished she could believe, a happy ending that gave the lie to reason and experience. In the same way she felt obscurely touched by Signora Donati's action as if she had said something kind but untrue.

Other than that one question about her mother, she hadn't pried into Rachel's life nor the nature of her relationship with her son beyond its obvious professionalism. Her movements, deliberate, measured, never fussy, possessed a capacity for stillness that Rachel recognized in Donati the first time she saw him on the steps of the church. The women Rachel saw in the church everyday were the same, the low recitation of prayers, the metallic chink as they dropped a coin in the poor box on their way out, the self-effacing, generous remembrance of another.

"Please thank her for me," she said at last.

Donati parked outside the courtyard, hefting Rachel's bag out of the back seat and carrying it up the steps, his other arm supporting her round the waist. Breathless with fatigue, Rachel unlocked the door, entering her apartment with relief, feeling like she'd been away for months.

"Is there anything you need?" Donati asked, putting her bag down on the bed.

"Just rest," Rachel replied. "I want to get an early start in the morning."

By the end of the following day they uncovered the third and final figure in the central panel. John the beloved disciple supporting Mary in his arms. Unlike Mary, it was not grief etched in the lines in his forehead, pulling down the corners of his mouth, but anger. And instead of focusing on his dead master, as Rachel expected, John's eyes were fixed firmly on Mary.

"I've seen that look before," Rachel said to Donati, driving back over the river into the Trastevere district. "In some museum, but not in a painting. In an Anglo-Saxon Psalter in the British Museum. Eleventh century. I forget the name. The face of John was almost exactly the same. Pia might know."

That evening, Donati had invited Nigel and Pia over to his apartment to celebrate Rachel's recovery and brainstorm about the triptych. Entering a tiled foyer flanked by a series of doors with numbers on them,

Rachel saw a spiral staircase with iron railings curving upwards.

"You've got to be kidding," she said. Although mostly healed, Rachel's energy was still negligible given the amount of blood she had lost. Some days it was all she could do to remain upright in front of the triptych.

"There's an elevator," said Donati, steering her towards an old-fashioned concertina gate Rachel had only seen in movies.

Located on the top floor, Donati's apartment was a penthouse studio with kitchen, bathroom, loft bedroom and a spacious rooftop courtyard opening off the living room through immense floor-to-ceiling windows. North lay Vatican City and the dome of St. Peter's; west an uninterrupted view over the roof-tops to the Janiculum and the Botanical Gardens, and beyond, high on a hill, the equestrian statue of Garibaldi looking down over the city.

"The view's amazing," Rachel said.

A city of icons, of effigies executed in stone and paint, brilliantly hued mosaics and bronze, Rome was a city of faces—the eyeless stare of emperors cautioning against hubris, the humorless countenance of the saints warning of the dangers of *vanitas*. Only the images of the Virgin set at street level over doorways, on the sides of buildings, bridges, were homely, accessible. Instead of looking down on the teeming streets, patronizing in her ageless serenity, she adorned bakeries, post offices, bistros, bestowing myriad benedictions on the everyday, the mundane. If St. Peter, virile, stern, was the patron saint of Vatican City, Mary was the mother of the Roman people, the people who filled the piazzas and the pews, who clustered around her statues lighting candles, reciting prayers.

Donati came up behind her, arms encircling her waist, a thing he did frequently in the chapel when he sensed her exhaustion. Gratefully, Rachel leaned into him, moving with the rise and fall of his breathing. "Make yourself at home," he said. "I'll get us a drink."

A black-and-white cat ran down the steps of the loft from the bedroom and jumped onto the sofa, its face splitting into an ecstatic grin as Rachel scratched it under the chin.

"That's Geronimo," Donati called from the kitchen. "Of indeterminate age and prodigious randiness. I suspect he's fathered half the cats in Rome." He emerged carrying a bottle and two glasses.

Settling in Rachel's lap, the cat began to knead her sweater with his paws, snagging the wool into tiny catches, his whole body shuddering with the vibration of his purr.

"I thought you told me that most of the cats in Rome were wild?"

"They are. Here." Handing her a glass of wine, he slouched in a chair opposite, legs stretched out with feet propped up on the coffee table between them. "He adopted me, not the other way round. Just showed up at the window one morning. Takes off from time to time, probably to sponge off some other poor bastard, but he always comes back."

"I'm surprised."

"That he always comes back? So am I, considering I often forget to feed him."

"No," Rachel said. "I'm surprised you like cats. Not to be sexist, but most men don't."

"T.S. Eliot did."

Rachel looked at him.

"You think all we Italians do is read Dante and Petrarch? I minored in European Lit. So yes, I've read Dante and Petrarch, but also a bunch of others. See for yourself."

A great many of the books that lined the bookcase along one wall were almost entirely devoted to collections of poems. She could even make out some of the titles; Goethe, Wordsworth, Yeats, Dylan Thomas, Baudelaire, all in their original languages. Besides the complete plays of Shakespeare, Chaucer's *Canterbury Tales* and Camus' *L'Etranger* and *La Peste*, the other volumes consisted mostly of art books.

"No Bertolt Brecht?" she said. "I thought he was a good socialist."

"On my bedside table," Donati replied. "Along with Marx and Trotsky. You should try them sometime. Beats the hell out of Valium."

"So," Rachel said, studying him. "Let's make some deductions here. You were doing a major in art, but switched to conservation to please your father because he considered science of more use to society. Am I right?"

"Very impressive, but you're hardly the one to talk. I saw your sketches of the chapel. It's obvious you had some kind of training."

"The Pratt Institute."

"I'm impressed."

"Don't be. I transferred in my second year."

"How come?"

"Good question," Rachel said, tickling Geronimo behind the ears, generating more stertorous purring.

"I've asked myself that many times. Funny, but my art professor never did."

Hearing her professor greet her as "Rachel" when she stuck her head round his door almost scared her off right then. She hadn't made an appointment, and he'd never used her first name before, preferring chilly formalities. When she told him she intended to switch, he didn't try to argue her out of her decision, nor question it, just signed the appropriate forms and handed them silently across the desk. Whenever they bumped into each other after that, he never referred to their meeting, reverting to Ms. Piers. She always felt grateful to him for that, like meeting a priest knowing he was bound by the seal of the confessional.

"I liked the idea of saving something from the past. You know," Rachel said, "being able to reverse the damage of time."

"Yes," he said, "The resurrection business, you and me both. And before you tell me that's a bit extreme, I know."

Sheathing and unsheathing his claws, the cat fixed her with a single yellow eye.

"I'm going to make a start on dinner," Donati said, heading into the kitchen. "If Geronimo becomes a nuisance, shove him outside."

He was standing at a chopping board, dicing vegetables and throwing them into a skillet when Rachel came in. Perching on a stool at the counter, she picked up a green pepper, split it with her fingers, and began to scoop out the seeds.

A buzzer sounded. Donati pressed an intercom on the wall. "*Pronto!*"

"We're here."

Donati put down the knife and wiped his hands on the front of his shirt. "Are you sure you're up for this?" he asked Rachel, covering the speaker with his hand. "They'll understand if you're too tired."

"Yes," she said. "We need to talk about the project, compare notes."

Gathered round the coffee table in the living room after dinner, Nigel and Pia were sitting side by side on the couch, Rachel lounging on the floor opposite, her back resting against Donati's knees while he sat in a chair behind her, every now and then, playing with strands of her hair.

"OK" Rachel said. "This is what we know: The triptych is almost certainly a Rogier." At her words Donati's fingers stilled momentarily, aware of the implications to the church and the impending loss of its icon, then resumed. Nigel and Pia sat silently, waiting for her to go on.

"Given the highly stylized depiction of Mary and John, the raw emotion, the pronounced aging of Mary, the almost sculptural solidity of the composition, I'd say it was painted very late in his career, 1450s or early '60s."

"The carbon dating is conclusive," Donati said.

"The use of 'dragon's blood' is troubling, though," Nigel said. "I know there was an embargo at the port due to plague, but I'm still not convinced Rogier would have employed such an unstable pigment."

"Maybe it was used by one of his assistants?" Pia put in.

139

"Hans Memling was Rogier's most promising pupil in the 1450s," said Donati. "His hand crops up everywhere during that period and he's notorious for his use of 'dragon's blood.'"

"True," said Rachel. "But there's no evidence of multiple styles, however closely they conform to Rogier's. The continuity of style in the evolution of drawing to finished painting is too consistent. Another artist's work would have shown up on x-rays, not to mention the infrared scans. Besides, Rogier would have retained absolute control over his materials."

"Agreed," Donati said. "But what about the frame? The wood analysis establishes that the panels were painted in Northern Europe but framed here; the notion that the frame is separate from the main panels is unusual."

Generally considered part of the entire design in medieval altarpieces, the frame's installation was carefully supervised by the artist himself. Only in the Renaissance era with the advent of humanist salons in powerful Italian families such as the Medicis and the Borgias, did the notion of a frame being primarily decorative and removable come into being.

"We know that Rogier visited Italy in 1450," Rachel said, "because many of his portraits date from after this time and we can track Italian influences. Pia, anything to indicate Rogier was connected to Our Lady of Sorrows in any way?"

"I haven't been able to turn anything up at the church," Pia said. "The monsignor's been helpful but the crypt's been flooded so many times the parish registers are virtually illegible. I'll keep digging."

"Then there's this odd connection to the convent and illuminated manuscripts," said Rachel. Pia's trip to Bruges had been fruitful, yielding a wealth of documentary evidence—bills of sale, ledger books meticulously kept in tiny, graceful script—that proved 'dragon's blood' had been purchased from a convent just outside the town. Called the "Convent of the Immaculate Conception," it had housed the sisters of the Poor Clares since the fifteenth century. The original building was still standing, Pia reported, though largely restored.

"The library's full of illuminated manuscripts," she said. "I've never seen anything like it, incredible realism, and many of them executed in the mid-fifteenth century by a young novice."

"That reminds me," Rachel said. "I'd like you to photograph the face of John on the central panel and see if you can match it stylistically to manuscript depictions. Try the data base of the British Museum beginning at Anglo-Saxon."

"Vellum not parchment, then," Pia said.

"Probably," said Rachel. "But you might want to check databases for both mediums." Waiting for Pia to finish jotting down notes, she shifted her weight against Donati's legs, feeling him stir fractionally to accommodate her new position.

"Perhaps we're getting sidetracked," she continued. "Maybe there's no connection between the triptych and the convent aside from it being a source of 'dragon's blood'?" Rachel looked at Pia. "Keep working on the church records. We need to find out when the triptych came to Rome and was installed. Focus on the date 1450. Also, find out more about the convent, see if we can't eliminate it from the puzzle, or to explain it somehow. Nigel, you're the expert on frames. Can you analyze the gold leaf and see if you can identify Rogier's application technique and materials, the caret of the gold and its thickness as well as the ground he used as an adhesive medium?"

"Will do."

"What about me?" Donati asked, tweaking a strand.

Tipping her head back, Rachel looked at him upside down. "You and I start on the side panels tomorrow."

XIX

"ARE YOU SURE YOU DON'T MIND GOING BACK?" Rachel and Pia were sitting on a bench in the Air Terminal on the Via Giolitte waiting for a bus to take Pia to Leonardo da Vinci.

"I'm sure," Pia said. "The convent library's a treasure trove for someone like me. Besides, the nuns spoil me, keep plying me with mead they make from honey from their beehives. They're famous for it."

Air brakes hissing, the bus swung round the corner and drew up alongside. Pia boarded at the rear while the new arrivals poured out the doors in the center, clustering in small groups on the sidewalk, dazed with jet lag.

"I'll call as soon as I turn up anything," Pia called through the door. "*Ciao.*"

After what she had seen in the lab this morning, Rachel decided to send Pia back to Bruges. She needed to satisfy herself that the convent connection was circumstantial. Glancing at her watch, she quickened her pace, taking the shortest route to the lab where Nigel worked.

Early that morning, she had been taking a bath when Nigel rang.

"How soon can you get here? We've just turned up something interesting."

"I can be at the lab by nine-thirty," she replied. When Nigel used the word "interesting," he meant extraordinary.

The new lab was on the sixth floor of a steel and glass high-rise on the other side of town.

"Welcome to the wave of the future," Donati said when Rachel met him inside the foyer. She shook the rain from her jacket, their feet leaving glistening smears on the black marble floor as they walked towards the elevators. "How are you feeling?"

"Like I could use a vacation."

"Amen to that," said Donati.

Rachel entertained a vision of them lying on a beach somewhere, heat permeating her aching body, the clash of palm trees in the wind, the rhythmic lap of water, the entire scene a perfect tourist brochure cliché, but one that appeared painfully attractive to her at that moment.

"You are now on the sixth floor," an electronic voice announced in Italian, banishing her guilty fantasy.

"I hate machines that talk," complained Donati as they exited the elevator, turning left down a long carpeted corridor towards a chrome door at the far end. "Conservation Center of Rome" the plaque read. They found themselves in another corridor identical to the one they had just left.

"This is it." Donati pushed open one of the doors. The sign read: '*Attenzione: x-rays.*'

Nigel and Pia were standing in front of an x-ray viewing screen where negatives of the right and left side panels were displayed. "There's something odd about the donor grouping," Nigel said.

"How many donors in all?" Rachel asked.

"Nine."

Rachel studied the negatives closely. The right panel showed a series of dark shapes lined up across the width of the film, bulkier than their counterparts on the other panel with dark lines descending and flowing out behind them.

"These must be the women. You can see the folds of their dresses, and they're wearing some kind of headdress."

"That's not unusual," Donati said

"Do you want to tell him or shall I?" said Nigel.

"The right side is usually reserved for the male donors," Rachel explained. "Women are generally depicted on the left." In medieval symbolism women, daughters of Eve, were always depicted on the left, a sign of their theologically inferior and socially subservient status in relation to men.

"*La sinistra*," Donati said, referring to the Latin for left. "They could be saints." In the absence of male saints, holy women took precedence on the right.

"Too many for a painting this small and there's no indication of other forms of identification," Rachel said. In the Baultenheimer Altarpiece St. Catherine was haloed by the wheel of her martyrdom. "Look at the descending order of size. My guess is this is a portrait of a mother and her four daughters."

"Except there are two missing." Donati tapped the film with a pencil. "Look at the gaps on this side, or to be exact, two fuzzy areas. Here, just behind the first figure.

And here, behind the third. There's no indication of this on the other panel, presumably the male family members."

"Damage?" Pia suggested.

Rachel shook her head. "There's nothing on the surface to suggest that. We know that at the time the triptych was painted lead was the primary ingredient of white paint and x-rays can't penetrate lead."

"Hence the dark areas," said Nigel. "What we're looking at are seven portraits executed almost exclusively in white, with two figures dressed in black or some other dark color." He was counting the four figures in the other panel that had also come up dark and blotchy.

"Rogier's diptych of the *Crucifixion* in the Philadelphia Museum of Art has John and Mary exclusively in white," Rachel said. "It's his last major composition, circa 1463, and we know he was influenced by the white habit of the Carthusian monastery at Herne where his son entered."

But the reverse positions of the male and female donors puzzled her, as did the extravagant use of white for the donors. She could hear the rain beating against the windows in blustery squalls, there would be a lull, then it would start up again like someone knocking to be let in.

If she included Mary's robe and the winding sheets draped around the dead Christ, that made eleven figures dressed in white. Given the medieval love of color and the fact that donors were usually sumptuously dressed to display their wealth and social status, she knew there must be some other symbolic reason. White was worn at funerals in ancient Rome, she knew, but by the Dark Ages on, it was customary for mourners to wear black out of respect for the pall draped over the coffin.

"Good morning, everyone!"

Persegati was standing in the doorway. "I would have been here earlier, but I had to attend a funeral." Dressed in a dark-colored suit with a white carnation in his buttonhole, he looked more like he'd come from a wedding than a funeral, Rachel thought.

His unexpected arrival meant he would have to be told his preliminary tests on the triptych were correct—they had almost certainly discovered a late, lost work by Rogier Van der Weyden.

XX

"HEY," DONATI SAID, walking into the chapel.

"That was a long break," Rachel said.

"Don't you want to know what I've been doing?"

"Not particularly."

"You're in a good mood."

"You'd be too if you had to work in this icebox all afternoon." She huffed out a cloud of breath. "If you'd arrived any later, you'd have found me frozen to the altar. The space heater packed up soon after you left."

"Cheer up," he said, catching up her hands and beginning to chafe them between his own. "While you've been being defeated by technology, I've been busy making it work in our favor." He reached inside his breast pocket and extracted a piece of paper. "I went over some of the infra-red results in case we missed anything the first time round," Donati said, handing her the paper. "As it happens, we did."

In the lower right-hand corner of the left panel, faint but unmistakable, were two letters—*A* and *D*.

She turned to the triptych and looked closely at the left panel.

"Don't bother," Donati said. "The letters were scratched into the gesso and then painted over. Even the raking light didn't pick them up."

"But why would anyone want to hide the symbols for 'Anno Domini'?" Rachel said, rubbing at her eyes, strained from too much close work on the panels.

"Come on," he said, pulling her to her feet and draping her coat round her shoulders. "Let's get out of here. You won't be able to figure it out tonight. You've had enough."

Too weary to resist, Rachel watched as he turned off the lights and locked up.

"What do you have in mind?" she asked.

"How about a movie," Donati said.

"I promised I'd call Pia."

"You can do that from the theater lobby."

"Sorry I'm late," whispered Rachel, sliding into the seat beside Donati at the movie theater. "It took me ages to get through to Pia." She didn't add that she had had to stand at the back of the movie theater for some time before she was able to pick him out of the crowd. In the end, it was his posture that tipped her off. He was sitting with his feet propped up on the back of the seat in front of him, the way he always sat on the prie dieux in the chapel whenever he took a break.

"Anything interesting?" He angled a box of popcorn towards her.

"She hasn't found anyone whose name corresponds to the initials, if that's what you mean," Rachel said, dabbling her fingers in the box. "But she did find out the name of the nun who did all those illuminations. Sister Magdalena. Apparently, she was incredibly prolific considering she died at the age of thirty-one."

"*Silencio*!" someone hissed.

Swiveling her head to the front, she tried to pick up the thread of the plot. Useless. The movie was halfway through and the clumsy dubbing of Italian over English was distracting, if not ludicrous. Some sort of ceremony was going on. She caught a glimpse of white lace. "What did you say this was called?" she whispered.

"*Four Weddings and a Funeral.* Why?"

"I've just figured something out."

"Anything to do with getting grease stains out of denim?"

"Sorry." She had inadvertently spilled the contents of the box in his lap.

"*Non importa.* Given any thought to dinner yet?"

"I'm afraid you're wearing it."

"Let's go."

Fortunately the movie theater was only a short distance from Donati's apartment. Stopping briefly to pick up pizza from a trattoria on the corner of Donati's street, they shared the elevator up with one of the other residents, a middle-aged man, his suit oddly paired with the motorcycle helmet he held under his arm. He smiled politely, getting out at the second floor.

"Right," Donati said, lighting up a cigarette. "Let's have it then." He flicked the spent match into the empty pizza box and leaned back, his arms straddling the back of his chair.

Rachel had kicked off her shoes and was lying stretched out on the sofa with a balloon glass of brandy balanced on her stomach.

"Mmm?" Drowsy and full of food, she was watching the liquid in her glass quiver each time she took a breath, a shimmer of amber.

"Something about weddings," he prompted.

"And a funeral," Rachel said, coming fully alert. "Do you remember what first tipped us off about the convent being the supplier of the 'dragon's blood'?"

"Plague."

"In other words, death, funerals."

"That's the usual order," Donati agreed. "But I still don't see what this has to do with the triptych."

"I'm getting to that. People usually wear black at a funeral, right? But yesterday, Persegati was wearing a white carnation in his buttonhole. He looked like he'd just come from a wedding."

"It's an ancient custom that dates back to the Romans," Donati said. "Black symbolizes mourning, white the hope of immortality."

"So when the triptych was painted, the donors dressed in white were already dead of the plague. Only the two women dressed in black survived. That's my theory."

"The triptych's some kind of memorial?"

"That's my guess. Now for the second part of my hunch, and this is going to be the trickiest to prove. My legal name before my divorce was Mrs. Mark Prescott III, right?"

"So?"

"In other words, not Piers. So what does a nun do when she enters a convent?"

"She changes her name."

"Why?"

"Because she becomes the bride of Christ. The ceremony is like a wedding," Donati said, "even down to a ring, vows and the traditional white."

"When a woman changes her maiden name, it's as if her old self ceases to exist. A sort of death, if you like."

"Dying to the world," Donati said. "So what you're saying is that the reason Pia can't match up the initials with this Sister Magdalena is because she changed her name when she took vows."

"We may not be able to prove any of it if Pia turns up a blank in the convent records."

"What about it being in Rome?" Donati said. "If it's a memorial to the painter's family, you'd think she'd want it to remain in Bruges."

"Unless the other sister moved away after her parents' death."

"Come to Rome, you mean?" He stared thoughtfully into his glass, swirling the contents around and around. "The only way a woman could have done that in those days was to marry an Italian."

"Pia could research the marriage records in the church." Rachel looked at her watch. Midnight. She swung her legs off the sofa.

"You don't have to go, you know," Donati said.

XXI

"The sun's shining."

Rachel peered at Donati's panel. "I don't see any sun."

"I mean outside, *stupida*."

A black spot, darker than the general pall which coated the rest of the panel, had refused to dissolve.

"Can you pass me that quill? I think it's in a box somewhere," Rachel said.

Donati rummaged in a shoe box, found the feather, and handed it to her. Rachel tested the point against the tip of her finger to make sure it would give before scratching the paint, then began to scrape very gently at the surface of the painting. A tiny shower of black grains fell onto the altar. She dabbed at them with the tip of her finger, rubbing them between finger and thumb. "Soot," she said. "And it feels greasy, not dry."

"Tallow. I'll get it analyzed." He scooped up a minute portion with a spatula and tipped it carefully into a bag. Turning back to the one-inch section she was working on, she carefully wiped at the upper right-hand corner. It revealed a patch of blue sky and the tip of a crenellated structure, almost certainly the tower of a castle.

"Don't you find that odd?" she said.

"That we're working and it's Saturday? Yes, as a matter of fact, I do."

"The structure," Rachel said pointing to the castle. "Rogier's later works almost never have intricate backgrounds. His earlier work like his *Adoration of the Magi* Altarpiece, yes, but his later works were so much starker, more minimalist and textured than this."

Donati sighed.

Rachel discarded the swab and reached for a fresh one. "You know we're behind schedule."

"We were here until midnight last night."

"Quit whining," Rachel said. "And do something useful for a change."

The next thing she knew his hands were straddling the small of her back. "You almost made me take off some paint," she said.

"You told me to do something useful." He dug his thumbs in hard.

"That hurts!"

"It's supposed to." His fingers switched to her shoulders, working out the accumulated tension of the last few weeks, the dull ache of the miscarriage, a pain that went deeper than her body. Rachel felt herself becoming slack under his hands, the strain draining away. Donati was right. She had been working flat out, barely taking time to eat, a way of dealing with her loss, and also because Persegati was getting impatient for results. The thought of playing truant for a day suddenly seemed immensely tempting.

"Got any ideas?" she murmured.

"Plenty," he said, brushing her hair aside so he could work on her neck. "Fancy going to the Villa Borghese Gardens?"

"I was thinking more of a nap."

"You can do that too."

When Donati invited her to spend the night at his place Rachel hesitated. The months before now seemed unreal, blurred, a distant horizon she was moving away from not towards. She could plot her new beginning from the moment she awoke in the hospital and the sound of Donati's breathing seemed as familiar as her own, an extension of the hours they had spent working on the triptych, shoulders bumping, hands moving in unison over the panels intent on their task. But the destination she was rushing towards was not yet fully defined; she wanted to slow down, feel her way more securely, pick through her emotions selectively. Her marriage and everything that had gone before made her shy of intimacy, distrustful of the everyday familiarity between lovers, horrified at the thought of another failure. There was too much she could learn that would disappoint her, too much Donati would learn.

In the end, he solved her uncertainty by the naturalness with which he put down his glass and switched the lights off one by one as if he were going through his nightly routine. His arm, when he held out his hand to her, showed black against the windows and the night beyond. The rooftops of Trastevere were inky squares patchworked over a darker sky filled with innumerable stars, bars of light gleamed here and there through shutters, a dog barked in the distance. His gesture, spanning the gap between them, between the past and the present, between this moment and the next, remained.

Rachel could see him looking at her from across the room, his gaze transfixing her, answering her own with devastating simplicity, drawing her into the place where he had been waiting, a place where she could know him and be known. For a moment they hung there, each regarding the other across a threshold of separateness, then the space between them shifted, dissolved, reformed into something wholly new as Rachel got up and went towards him.

They were sitting on a blanket in the Piazza di Siena, an eighteenth century amphitheater in the middle of the Villa Borghese Gardens. Rachel had given in, partly because she wanted to think over the puzzling inconsistency of the background with Rogier's late style, partly because she longed to feel the sun on her face after so many months of winter. The remains of a picnic lay scattered on the grass at their feet. At Rachel's suggestion, they had invited Angelo along.

"There," Rachel said, plaiting grass into a coronet and placing it on Angelo's head. He was sitting cross-legged on the grass following the movement of her fingers raptly. From time to time his hand strayed to his head where his crown was in danger of slipping over his eyes.

"*Grazie*," he said. Since her miscarriage he had taken to following her around the church, a devoted acolyte ready to hand her a fresh swab or fetch her coffee from the nearby cafe. Donati told her that something about the night of the miscarriage had convinced him Rachel was someone to be trusted, that he had doubtless picked up on the new closeness between her and Donati. For her part, Rachel found herself bringing Angelo simple gifts— a pen she had somehow acquired with a tiny plastic Statue of Liberty on the cap, a scarf in the colors of his favorite soccer team purchased with Donati's help when they were browsing in a market one late Sunday afternoon. All but convinced that the triptych was a Rogier and would soon be removed from the church, Rachel felt her reciprocation a sham, a way of salving her conscience against the inevitable. Her offer to bring Angelo with them today was doubtless tinged with the same guilt. But today, at least, she would not allow herself to dwell on that, to remember that once the triptych was finished she would be returning to New York.

Rachel was lying on her stomach, chin cupped in her hands. They had found a spot beneath an umbrella pine on a gentle incline overlooking the amphitheater. Others had done the same and blankets dotted the grass, tiny islands floating on a great expanse of green. Somewhere a cheap transistor was blaring out the local soccer match and a group of youths playing Frisbee on the plain below sent up a ragged cheer.

Donati was stretched out on his back beside her, propping himself on his elbows, head tipped back to the sun. Behind him a row of poplars cut the sky with piercing clarity, steepled summits swaying imperceptibly in the breeze. About them the ground was littered with pine cones and a thick yielding of needles softened by months of frost and rain. Sparrows, finches, birds she had not noticed before, darted amongst the branches, released from their drab hibernation as all around her

Rome shook off its inertia, rousing itself after the long, deadening sleep of winter and unfurling to the sun.

"You know what this reminds me of?" she said.

"Mmm?"

"A Breughel painting."

"More like Bosch's *Garden of Earthly Delights*," he said. "The Borgheses were a pretty sensual bunch."

"I mean ordinary people taking pleasure in simple things."

The sky over the piazza was deep aqua, scoured of clouds by a freshening breeze. A kite hung there, streamers snapping and fluttering in the wind as it climbed higher, the string attached to the base now taut, now slack, skillfully controlled by a boy in the center of the amphitheater.

Angelo ran off towards it. Dressed in jeans and sweatshirt, he looked more like a normal boy than Rachel had ever seen him, jumping down the stone steps two at a time like a nine-year-old. Slowly the kite nosed upwards, rising and dipping as it searched for the stronger currents that would keep it aloft.

"Don't go far," Donati shouted after him. Then, turning to Rachel, "So what were you saying about the background in the chapel?"

"It doesn't fit with Rogier's late style," she said. "The detail's too fine, too architecturally precise. In his later works he's more interested in reducing his narrative to a minimum, focusing in on its symbolic import via color, positioning, dimensional layering of figures. That's consistent with the central panel. After 1450 he's more and more interested in the figures in his narratives, less in the verisimilitude of their surroundings, probably because he became unofficial court painter to Philip the Good after Van Eyck's death. The side panels seem an anomaly somehow."

"Is there a chance they were painted by one of his assistants, someone whose style is virtually indistinguishable but whose compositional skills are inferior?"

"You tell me," Rachel said. "You did the tests. There's no appreciable difference in texture, pigment, no under-modeling, no *pentimenti,* no indication whatsoever that the side panels were painted by a different artist, and like I said before, I'd recognize Hans Memling's style anywhere. He's the only one of Rogier's assistants who could have approximated his master's style, and even then, he was too much of a genius himself not to be distinctive."

Donati picked up a handful of pine needles and let them blow through his fingers. "So where does that leave us exactly?"

"Back to square one with a Rogier oddly uncharacteristic of his mature style in essential elements. I don't know," Rachel said, rolling onto her back and putting her arm over her eyes to block out the sun, now past its zenith and beginning to dip into the West. "I can't seem to get a grip on this one. And so much depends on a conclusive identification."

"As far as Persegati's concerned, the identity of the painter is conclusive."

"Persegati can go to hell," Rachel said. "I want all the facts before I make that judgment and we're not there yet."

Donati shifted closer, his body suddenly warming the side where the shadows were beginning to reach, now the sun was going down. "You know identifying a Rogier would be career making."

Rachel squinted at him from beneath her arm. "I know," she said. "What are you getting at?"

"Only that if it's not a Rogier the chances of it being someone as famous are next to nil."

"So?"

Donati was looking ahead, still watching Angelo and the boy with the kite. "So I'm saying why not leave it at that. Persegati's convinced he's got what he wanted. Apex will be happy. Your career will be made. There isn't a museum that wouldn't hire you. You could take your pick."

The sounds of the park receded; Rachel was vaguely aware that people were beginning to gather their things together in preparation for going home, that the air had turned chilly as the shadows lengthened, that the boy with the kite had gone and Angelo was beginning to walk back towards them. There was something infinitely tempting about what Donati had said; not only would it resolve her current dilemma but it would ensure promotion to chief conservator, a position Rachel had coveted all her professional life. That Donati was willing to suggest such a thing made her reel, not only because it went against everything he believed, but because it was a decision he had not hesitated in making. She knew in an instant that his words were more compelling than any Hallmark formulation of love and that her refusal to go along with them would be the same.

They followed a path out of the park angling roughly south west along the Viale dei Papazzi then turned right towards an ornamental lake where the Temple of Aesculapius stood on a small island. Ducks clustered at the railings along the muddy bank leaving a white swan to cruise the lake in solitary possession. Donati handed Angelo some leftover bread from the picnic, and he ran on ahead, a raucous cacophony greeting him as he flung pieces, sometimes accurately, sometimes not, into the milling squabble. Rachel and Donati caught up with him and stood watching, huddled close. Donati's right arm was around her waist under her jacket, his fingers tucked into the waistband of her jeans, his thumb moving in spirals over the small of her back. Rachel leaned against him, her left arm slung around his shoulder, the blanket they had been sitting on folded and draped over her right arm. Since their conversation about the triptych, a quietness had descended on them, one redolent with a subtext only they could read. A pact had been made, one that committed them to following the triptych wherever it might lead, down a way they might not otherwise have chosen, their time together a thing to be attended to without the distraction of words. The ethereal whiteness of the temple rising out of the darkening lake, the burnt cinnabar of the sky behind it, the single swan, momentarily framed by the columns, all were details that coalesced and fixed themselves into permanence as Rachel looked at them, memories stored against the time when she would be gone.

Donati had parked his friend's car along the Viale Washington, the main thoroughfare dividing the Villa Borghese from the Pincio Gardens to the west. They drove down the hill, under the classical gateway on the Piazzale Flaminio, into the wide circular sweep of the

161

Piazza del Popolo. Donati negotiated the lanes of traffic rotating around the hub of the piazza where they branched off into three streets leading south into the heart of the city, then swung right along the central Via del Corso between the baroque churches of Santa Maria dei Miracoli and Santa Maria in Montesanto. Lighted storefront windows zipped past, yellow tracers flickering in Rachel's peripheral vision, creating an illusion of speed impossible on such congested roads. Donati made another right, skirted the decaying mound of Augustus' Mausoleum and picked up the Via di Ripetta that would take them more nearly into the part of the city where the church stood.

It was fully dark when they dropped Angelo back off at the church in time for the vigil Mass. Before getting out of the car, he leaned over the front passenger seat where Rachel was sitting and kissed her on the cheek. "*Grazie*," he said, a word he had repeated with increasing solemnity throughout the day. "*Grazie.*"

"I'll meet you in the chapel," Rachel called as Donati accompanied Angelo to the rectory door at the side of the church. "I need to get my computer."

She pushed open the main doors and entered quietly. Confessions were just ending and a boy she didn't recognize was lighting candles on the altar. A woman passed her trailing a small child by the hand. She dipped her fingers briefly in the holy water stoup at the door, crossed herself then sketched a cross on the forehead of the child with her thumb. The child rubbed the unexpected wetness petulantly, then put his fingers in his mouth.

Although Rachel had remembered to turn off the lights when she left, the gate to the chapel was unlocked and she had forgotten to cover the panels with plastic sheeting. A quick glance around told her that nothing had been disturbed. Her computer was under one of the kneelers, its hum unnaturally loud, batteries low. She turned it off. On an impulse, she lined up the votive candles in front of the triptych, lit them, then sat down on a chair in the center of the chapel.

Apart from the paraphernalia of the restoration process, arc-lights, swabs, bottles of solvent, brushes, the chapel looked much as it had done the first time she saw it except that now the painting was almost fully revealed, the living light giving an illusion of movement and dimensionality to the white cloths covering the dead Christ on the central panel and the donors' clothing on the side panels. Parchment pale, an exact reflection of the pallor of Christ's corpse with an almost complete absence of flesh tones and shading, the faces of all but two of the donors appeared mask-like, stiff, the eyes flat as if they were not only witnesses but participants in the drama being enacted on the central panel. Only Mary and John in the center panel, and one of the women in the right panel evinced a spark of human emotion, a mobility of feature that communicated grief, anger, stunned incomprehension.

Unlike the rest of the family, two of the female donors were dressed in black, one kneeling directly behind an older woman, the mother, the other placed conventionally behind her sister in descending order of age. Rachel had not yet finished cleaning the upper torso and face of the younger of the two but there was an odd twist of the body towards the viewer, a divergence in the flowing verticality of the bodice that suggested a different posture, one of confrontation, even agitation.

Rachel could not account for this strange disruption in the emotional decorum of the grouping, this odd singling out of one over the rest. In portraiture the engagement of the viewer by the subject was expected, but in devotional paintings such a compositional technique ran the risk of taking the focus off the central panel where the attention of the viewer was invited to dwell undisturbed on the theological significance of the biblical scene. Ultimate viewers, donors were supposed to be passive adjuncts to the main drama, not central players.

Combined with the stricken tone of the entire composition, this aberration gave the triptych a complicated, almost mystical allure which worked strangely on Rachel as she sat quietly in the chapel. An event that should have been fixed in time and space, the *Lamentation* sent shock waves through every aspect of human life and the bloodlines that stretched along the generations into the future. If any grace could be gleaned from such tragedy, Rachel could not discern it. Hidden in the heart of the church, she sat on, strangely moved by the honesty of the painting, by the observation of a painter too bleak and uncompromising to offer the comfort of conventional pieties.

XXII

THE PACE OF THE RESTORATION HAD PICKED UP since Pia's return from Bruges. A few days ago Rachel and Donati completed work on the triptych, and Nigel was almost finished cementing hairline cracks in the frame and touching up the gold leaf. Evenings were spent at Donati's apartment going over slides and discussing the order in which Rachel would present their findings at the press conference scheduled for that evening. Extraordinarily bold for a last major work, the gender reversal of the donor grouping, the symbolic meaning of the white clothing, were now explained. The link between the donors and the painter, the last, clinching piece of the puzzle, had been supplied by Pia.

She spent the morning going over her notes making sure she hadn't missed anything. The panels now formed a coherent tableau, remarkable not only for the dramatic contrast between the reds and whites, the foreground and the background, but by the historical narrative behind the painting, a story Rachel now knew in full.

What had at first appeared to be a castle behind the female donors, had turned out to be an extensive turreted structure, bluish in the distance, surrounded by fields and orchards laid out in grids along the sloping hills. Set out in a row beneath the trees of one of the orchards, a close inspection revealed a series of tiny cone-shaped beehives, their basketry so exquisitely rendered, the pattern and texture of the weaving was clearly visible. But what chiefly drew the eye was the third female donor whose shoulders and head were turned outwards from the painting towards the viewer in what could only be described as a stark face to face confrontation. Not only was her posture a bold break in accepted protocol for the depiction of donors, but the complexity and directness of her expression was unprecedented in Rachel's experience. The concentration of personality in a female face was much less common than in male portraits, no doubt accounting for the enduring fascination with the enigmatic expression of Leonardo da Vinci's *Mona Lisa*. Women were usually depicted displaying muted, even simplified, emotions contingent on an obvious male counterpart—the devotion of a wife, the grief of a mother, the docility of a daughter. Seldom did the expression on the face of a female figure emanate solely from the complexity of her own unique personality and particular experience. To invite the viewer to puzzle over a female face like this, to try to understand its passionate ambiguity, its obvious challenge, was not only rare it was revolutionary. Rachel now knew the reason for this.

By contrast, the male donors were depicted conventionally against a city skyline of what was undoubtedly medieval Bruges, its link to their occupation and social standing in the wealthy merchant class unremarkable except for the uniform whiteness of their attire.

Satisfied she had left nothing crucial out of her presentation, that her evidence unfolded with irrefutable logic and persuasion, Rachel closed up her computer and left the *pensione*. Instead of going directly to the church via the Piazza Navona, Rachel took a more circuitous route east through the S. Eustachio district to the Pantheon, north through the Piazza Minerva, then left at the church of S. Maria Maddelena to the Via della Scrofa and the church of Sant' Agostino. By approaching the church where the triptych was located from a different direction, by deliberately changing the sights and sounds of her morning walk, Rachel consciously prepared herself for departure. Recognized and hailed by shopkeepers in the neighborhood where she lived, by the women who cleaned the steps of their homes each morning, she had allowed herself to be lulled into a false sense of belonging. By coming at the church from the north instead of the south, she began the difficult task of severing her connection to it.

It was well after rush hour, and the sun had climbed high enough to burn off the early chill and clotheslines appeared over the alleys in readiness for the day's washing. Except for children shouting at play, the side streets were relatively quiet until she turned into the Via dell' Orso. Here upholsterers, jewelers, carpenters, gilders and a variety of other crafts were crammed along the entire length of the street, their doors open as much as to admit the mild spring air as to entice prospective buyers.

Inside an upholstery shop a woman was haggling with a tired-looking shop keeper over the price of cloth. After a rapid exchange, the man placed his right index finger on the skin under his eye and pulled down slightly to signify that an agreement had been reached. As money changed hands, the woman looked satisfied, the man mournful.

Rachel stopped at the end of the street. It was after ten and she had skipped breakfast. A sign that read "*Salumeria*" caught her eye so she crossed the street towards it.

Ten minutes later, a roll and a Styrofoam cup of *cafe e latte* in her hand, she emerged from the deli and walked to a small piazza near Sant' Agostino, sitting down on the steps of the church. It was exactly as she remembered it from the time she had come to Rome to complete some research in the Angelica Library several years ago. Each afternoon she spent the siesta hour browsing in the antiquarian bookshops that crowded the neighborhood. While the shopkeepers dozed on their stools behind the counters, she leafed through volume after volume, sometimes reading whole chapters but mostly looking at engravings and black-and-white prints of old masters. That year the summer was sweltering, the darkened interiors soporific with the smell of old paper and warm leather. It was on one of those sleepy afternoons with the sun turning the dust motes to gyres of gold she had come across an original etching by the eighteenth century architectural artist Giovanni Battista Piranesi pressed between two layers of frayed cardboard. It now hung above her bed in her Manhattan apartment.

She drained her cup, tossing the last of the roll to the pigeons chuckling and strutting on the pavement at her feet. No one called out to her, no one waved, as she made her way to the church, but once inside she knew her brief moment of detachment would be gone. Donati would be waiting for her, and Angelo. Sitting outside on Donati's rooftop balcony hearing the noises of the street going on below, feeling the weight of his arm across her hip as they lay curled up together, Rachel molded against the warm length of him, watching the sun come up over Trastevere, the church bells announcing the beginning of the day, all these things Rachel could not imagine living without.

XXIII

"You'll do fine," Donati said as the taxi pulled up outside the Ferrara Museum.

Rachel nodded, her mouth dry.

Pia waited for them at the curb. Taking a deep breath, Rachel linked her arm through Donati's and the three of them walked up to the front doors.

A long mahogany table laden with crystal and silverware ran almost the entire length of the library, while tucked discreetly away in an alcove, a string quartet filled the room with the stately sequences of *Pachelbel's Canon*. Presiding above it all, flattered by the light of crystal chandeliers, the voluptuous body of Venus bestowed her benediction on the glittering event with evident relish.

"Ah, Dr. Piers, Donati!" Persegati was advancing towards them. "I want you to meet a friend of mine."

"*Coraggio*," Donati whispered, before turning and disappearing through the main doors.

Rachel allowed Persegati to draw her across the room. While she mingled, Donati, Pia and Nigel arranged to organize the equipment necessary for her presentation.

"May I introduce Monsignor Corolli of the Vatican Museums," said Persegati. "Monsignor, Dr. Rachel Piers."

"Charmed," the monsignor said, bowing. "I must congratulate you on your outstanding work."

"Thank you," Rachel replied. "The triptych is certainly unique."

"Unique? I would have thought it typical of Rogier's mature style."

"I think what Dr. Piers means," Persegati said, "is that with as great a genius as Rogier's, it is impossible not to use the term unique."

"Tell me, monsignor" Rachel said. "What precisely is your connection with Apex?"

"Why do you ask?"

"I was just curious how the Church feels about the steady drain on its religious heritage by the corporate sector."

His eyes serious, candid now the social pretenses had dropped away, the monsignor excused themselves to Persegati and beckoned her to a chair at the far end of the room.

"Dr. Piers," he said in a low voice, "I will be frank with you. I too am concerned about the way in which our churches are being gutted of their artworks. We have both dedicated our lives to preserving religious art; you in your capacity of conservator, mine as curator. Now, I know we approach the heritage of faith in a different way. You are more concerned with its historical import, whereas I am chiefly concerned with its spiritual content."

"The successful marriage between church and state."

"Precisely," the monsignor said. "And, like any marriage, this relationship should rightfully be kept in perfect balance. Neither one side nor the other should gain the upper hand, don't you agree?"

"What are you saying?"

"Simply this: the involvement of Apex has upset this delicate balance. What happens here tonight with the Rogier will set the precedent for a wholesale, shall we say, *borrowing*."

"That's a nice way of putting it," Rachel said.

"Perhaps you are not aware how the Ferrara Museum's agreement with Apex works," the monsignor said. "In return for the restoration of one of its most celebrated works—and, as you know, despite the poverty of some of the lesser known churches, most of them seem to have at least one masterpiece, albeit in abysmal condition due to pollution, neglect, time, vandalism—the church in question agrees to release the art to the Ferrara Museum for a limited period of, say, a year.

"All of this seems above board, of course, and in a way it is. The loaning out of art works is common practice. But my concern is this: that during that agreed upon year exhibited in the Ferrara Museum, cleverly arranged to placate the Roman state and the Tourist Board, the work will then be sent on an extensive international tour which, of course, generates considerable press coverage, not to mention revenues. None of which, I hasten to add, goes to relieve the original church."

"I see," Rachel said. "Not theft but a type of usury. Skim off the profit, then return the work to the church when its immediate value is exhausted."

"Except that the political, cultural and corporate kudos a painter as celebrated as Rogier will generate, will mean the chances of the work being returned are slim, if not nonexistent."

"So Persegati is a kind of broker," Rachel said, "identifying prospective pieces for corporate funding, backing them up with preliminary tests to ensure quality, then contacting anyone who would have the resources to pay for restoration—in this case, Apex—and arranging the exhibitions."

The monsignor nodded. "In return, the Ferrara Museum gets considerable press coverage and the particular corporate sponsor acquires a reputation as a patron of the arts, which in turn brings enormous cultural prestige. Fujifilm's sponsorship of the restoration of the Sistine Chapel a number of years ago is a very similar type of arrangement, with the exception that the paintings couldn't be moved, of course, and there was nothing unethical about their involvement. The difficulty is that nothing Persegati is doing is actually illegal. Irreligious, yes. Morally suspect, certainly."

Rachel was silent for a while. "Did you have anything to do with that reporter who showed up a couple of months ago asking questions?" she said at last.

"One of my more clumsy attempts to stir things up by exposing the link between Persegati's interests and Apex, I'm afraid. Corelli said you stonewalled him so we couldn't run with it."

"I would have appreciated a direct approach," Rachel said. "You could have told me all this then."

"I couldn't be sure if you were involved or not."

"I would have thought my paper and my work on the Baultenheimer Altarpiece indicated where my loyalties lie when it comes to religious art."

"You're right, Dr. Piers. Please accept my apology."

A waiter drifted past, carrying a tray of wine glasses, offering it first to Rachel, then to the monsignor. Rachel declined. Filled with Armani suits, Versace evening gowns, the laughter pitched a little too loud to be genuine, the room was reminiscent of numerous black tie dinners she attended with Mark at some gallery opening or other.

"I think I've found a way of making this whole issue academic," she said, finding an unexpected relief in openly disavowing Apex to the monsignor. "If you talk to my colleague Giovanni Donati over there, he has a press release summarizing the upcoming presentation. Corelli has also been given one. I think you will find it makes my position clear."

"Of course."

"In return, a favor." Rachel took a business card from her purse and wrote down Pia and Donati's names and telephone numbers on the back. Nigel, she knew, would soon be returning to his position at the National Gallery and his seniority would make him immune from any professional backlash. "These are the names of my colleagues, both of whom are superb at what they do. I would ask you to see what you can do for them in the conservation department of the Vatican Museums, if they should ever approach you after this evening."

The monsignor took the card and slipped it into his pocket. "Consider it done."

XXIV

"LADIES AND GENTLEMEN," Persegati said, tapping his coffee spoon on the side of his glass until the room fell silent. "I propose a toast." He stood up and lifted his glass. "To Brad Phillips of the Apex Corporation, without whose generous support we would not have been able to celebrate one of the most remarkable art discoveries this century."

"To the Apex Corporation," the room echoed, looking at the American seated on Persegati's right.

"Thank you," Phillips said, rising. "But the credit should rightfully go to Dr. Piers and her team of experts." He bowed towards her and raised his glass. "Ladies and gentlemen, I give you Dr. Rachel Piers."

Rachel acknowledged the sputter of applause with a brief nod.

"I don't want to upstage Dr. Piers, so I'll be brief. Apex is a world leader in the field of philanthropy. We believe in investing in community. We employ nearly fifty thousand people worldwide, many of them from the disadvantaged classes in undeveloped countries. This historic unveiling tonight is merely the latest in our charitable endeavors.

"So now, ladies and gentlemen, I give you another toast." Phillips waited for the scraping of chairs to subside as people stood up. "To the renaissance of patronage in our culture. To the continued collaboration between the Apex Corporation and the Ferrara Museum. To art."

Now the moment was upon her, Rachel felt supremely calm. As she picked up her notes and walked towards the screen set up at one end of the library, she visualized the triptych, its breathtaking unity of form, the audacity of the painter's intent, its ascetic, though profound, spiritual charism. When the lights dimmed and the image of the panels blazed into life behind her, the room seemed to still into the hallowed space of the chapel, its occupants poised, expectantly, for revelation.

"We have all come here tonight to witness the unveiling of a lost work by one of the greatest medieval painters. To quote the head of restoration at the Pratt Institute: 'Each painting is unique and contains the secret of its own history.' In order to lay bare this secret, we must be able to piece together clues in order to see, if you'll excuse the pun, the big picture.

"But what may at first appear to be the truth may turn out to be quite otherwise and the prudent conservateur learns to keep an open mind.

"As you can see, the panels were completely overlaid with dirt. We began by removing it with alkaline wax. Beneath that we uncovered a layer of varnish that had yellowed with age and which considerably distorted the original color of the pigments underneath. This we removed with a solution of acetone dissolved in white spirit.

"I won't bore you with the technical details, but I would like to tell you something about the painting itself. It was undoubtedly executed in the 1450s when Rogier was at peak production. The carbon 14 dating is highly accurate and the stylistic signature of Rogier is unmistakable."

Rachel indicated the central panel. "Note the emotion on the faces of Mary and John, their extraordinary *compassio*. Many of you will recognize these same expressions from other works by Rogier. His *Crucifixion Diptych*, circa 1455, being perhaps the most famous example, as well as the later *Crucifixion* in the Monastery of the Escorial in Spain.

"Also note the swooning posture of the Virgin. Rogier was the first to attribute bodily weakness to the Mother of God and it was revolutionary at the time. Why? Because, unlike his colleague Jan van Eyck, Rogier was less interested in painting a symbolically coherent, biblical narrative than in making a direct appeal to the emotions of the viewer. Instead of a static icon he gives us a real flesh and blood woman. As such we are able to directly identify with her grief at the loss of her child."

She made an *S* shape with the tip of the pointer, following the sinuous lines of Mary's robe. "Notice the rhythmic linear patterns in the folds of the cloth. The distortion of perspective and the illusion of movement is intended to instill a subconscious feeling of unease in the viewer. Again, what the painter is aiming for is a direct appeal to the emotions of the viewer. As I have said,

Rogier's hallmark is in the subjective rendering of his compositions, a lesser artist would have been content to confine this effect solely to the expressions on his character's faces. Not so with Rogier. As we have already seen, he preferred to convey emotion through a sense of movement and the calculated dislocation of perspective."

The next slide showed the male donors on the left hand panel.

"Ladies and gentlemen, I'd like to introduce you to Master Piert van Dykhuizen and his three sons. As you can see from the fur-lined, velvet cloak and the heavy gold chain around his neck, he was a wealthy man. He was, in fact, a merchant 'prince' specializing in the export of spices, raw silk, precious jewels and other such luxuries. He was well-known at the court of the Duke of Burgundy, and we know that he knew Rogier personally. So well, in fact, that he persuaded Rogier to take one of his daughters on as an apprentice painter."

Rachel saw Persegati and Brad Phillips exchange looks. Donati had positioned himself directly opposite her at the far end of the table with Nigel and Pia seated on either side. It was too dark to make out his expression, but the massing of his body against the light from the half-open door remained perfectly still, and she knew his eyes had not left her face.

"Considering the social constrictions on women at the time, not only was this an unheard of act of generosity on Rogier's part, it was almost scandalous, and one he never would have made had he not recognized in the girl the makings of a master painter.

"You'll also notice the landscape behind the male donors on this panel," Rachel said, clicking to the next slide which showed a close-up of the background. "We were able to confirm it as being an historically accurate panorama of medieval Bruges by comparing it to similar landscapes in a variety of works executed around the same period."

She returned to the slide showing the male donors.

"But why the white? Surely, a wealthy burgher would prefer to be depicted in brilliant colors more in keeping with his eminent social status? That puzzled me too until we realized that at the time the triptych was completed, Piert van Dykhuizen and most of his family were dead from the plague; thus white symbolizes the color of immortality.

"We were able to connect the plague epidemic to the liberal use of 'dragon's blood' in the painting, the only red pigment available due to an embargo at the ports."

Rachel indicated the rust-colored patches on the body of the dead Christ.

"It seemed strange to us that Rogier, knowing the inherent vice of this pigment, the fact that it was chemically unstable and would rapidly oxidize to a much deeper shade, should have gone ahead and used it rather than wait for the embargo to be lifted. The only reason for him to do so would either be that the triptych was commissioned by the donors for a certain date, or if delay were not possible for some other reason."

The next slide showed the female donors on the right panel. "I say *most* of the family died of the plague because we know two survived." She pointed to the figures dressed in black. "Adrianna van Dykhuizen and Saskia Facio."

179

She indicated the woman with a pensive expression, kneeling directly behind her mother, hands conventionally joined in prayer.

"Saskia married Bartolomeo Facio shortly before this painting was executed but moved to Rome soon after its completion. Many of you will be familiar with Bartolomeo's account of the painter Gentile da Fabriano in his work *De viris illustris* written in 1456. In this work he mentions that Rogier made a trip to Rome in 1450."

Picking up on the significance of the date, Persegati suddenly leaned forward in his chair.

Rachel pointed to the other sister dressed in black, the one turned to the viewer. Even now, separated by centuries, the strength of Adrianna's gaze had the power to reach into the room, commanding a response.

Beneath the gauze veil that floated above the fashionably shaved eyebrows and broad expanse of forehead, was a face of uncommon intelligence and character, the mouth wide, sensual, the gray eyes fixed on the viewer with an expression that rivaled John's for its fierceness, as if she would have liked to tell God exactly what she thought of him for allowing his Son and her family to die so miserably, so arbitrarily.

Rachel paused to take a sip of water. It was not nervousness that made her mouth dry now but the effort of projecting her voice in that large room. Her whole attention was taken up with the story she was narrating, a story and an extraordinary talent that had been hidden for centuries. By the stillness in the room, she could tell her audience was similarly caught up.

"At first, we could find no documentary evidence to tell us what happened to Adrianna after 1450. The only clue lay in the painting itself, a clue that only came to light once we fully uncovered the background behind the female donors.

"You will notice that the landscape painted in behind the female figures is not an urban one. In fact, it is a part of the countryside just outside Bruges. And if you look very closely, you will see a structure that looks, at first glance, to be a castle.

"It is, in fact, the Convent of the Immaculate Conception where Adrianna was professed a postulant the same year her sister moved to Rome. We know this from a register kept in the convent library that documents the names of all the nuns living there since its founding.

"Adrianna, or Sister Magdalena as we should now call her, was an artist in her own right. After taking the veil she dedicated her life to illuminating the Bible and the lives of the saints as befitted a pious nun who had forsaken the world for a life of prayer. The convent still possesses a handful of these manuscripts in its library. Not only did she work in the *illuminarium,* she spent the year of her novitiate completing her last great work. *This* last great work."

Rachel could feel her throat straining as she pitched her voice to carry to the reporters at the back of the room. "The so-called Rogier in the chapel here in Rome is an almost exact replica of the painting you now see before you. I say 'almost exact' because, aside from its size, there are several other important discrepancies."

This time the slide showed a blown-up image of the right panel of the triptych in Our Lady of Sorrows in Rome. Rachel pointed to a window in one of the turrets of the convent. Looking out was the face of a woman enclosed in a nun's wimple.

"This, ladies and gentlemen, is Sister Magdalena. If you compare her to the donor grouping, you will see that it is the same woman. The triptych in the chapel here in Rome was a wedding present to her sister, a gift that Rogier himself carried to Rome in 1450. More importantly, it was intended as a memorial to their family." She flipped to the altarpiece in Bruges. "As you can see, the convent window in this painting has no face at the window because the woman herself resided there and there was no need for a pictorial reminder of her vocation.

"In addition, the altarpiece in Bruges bears Adrianna's complete signature, whereas the one in Rome bears only her initials—*A. D.* At first, we thought these letters referred to the standard byline '*Anno Domino,*' a phrase commonly used by painters to indicate the date of the work. But what puzzled us was not only the lack of any such date, but the concealment of the letters under the layers of paint. Only when Pia tracked down the former name of Sister Magdalena, linking it to pictorial proof of Adrianna's identity in the paintings themselves, did the significance of the letters as a form of abbreviated signature become apparent.

"Then there was the question of the wood used to frame the triptych here in Rome. I must credit Giovanni Donati with this discovery. The wood is poplar, which as many of you know, was the type most commonly available in southern Europe, particularly the region surrounding Rome. In the colder climate of northern Europe, hard woods such as oak or walnut were routinely used because they were cheaper and resisted damp and subsequent warping much more efficiently.

"It follows, then, that Rogier delivered only the panels of the triptych to Saskia. Their framing was completed after she arrived in Rome with her new husband. My colleague Pia Amata, who specializes in historical documentary research, traced the date of installation of the triptych Adrianna gave to Saskia to the chapel in Our Lady of Sorrows. In the documents, it stipulates that it was intended as a gift in return for the constant prayers of the faithful for the souls of the Van Dyckhuizen family.

"Rogier could not have executed this work because he was not in Bruges during the time of its execution but traveling in Italy, visiting Florence and Venice, and eventually coming to Rome. In fact, I speculate it was he who personally oversaw the installation of the triptych and some of the final touches. There are certain idiosyncrasies in the laying on of the gold leaf, identified by my colleague Nigel Thompson, that lead us to suspect his hand.

"In conclusion, Adrianna van Dyckhuizen, one of the most accomplished and, undeniably, one of the most overlooked painters of her era, clearly intended her last public work to be an object of devotion, a lasting testament to the family she had lost and the talent she was prepared to give up in order to live a life of prayer. Surely we have a responsibility to ensure that her original intention is honored, if for no other reason than that the people of the parish of Our Lady of Sorrows can continue to find the solace her vision of suffering tempered by faith brings to their lives."

XXV

THE MOON RODE HIGH OVER THE PIAZZA in a cloudless sky, silvering the portico of Our Lady of Sorrows and the columns beneath. Ablaze with lights, its pews packed with people, the church was completely transformed from the one Rachel had come to know. Instead of the shabby building huddled in the corner of one of the smallest piazzas in Rome, the church was resplendent as a basilica, its classical facade graceful and serene, its interior jeweled with light.

The scent of incense perfumed the air as Rachel moved closer, mingling with the acrid smell of a dying bonfire in front of the steps. Donati was sitting on the steps waiting for her, just as he had been the first time they met. She moved quietly to his side. The monsignor's voice carried beyond the church into the square, each word enunciated so clearly it fell like a discrete drop of rain, translucent, perfect, weighted with faith.

The power of this holy night dispels all evil. Washes away guilt, restores lost innocence.

And now the words were not drops of water falling singly but beads of mercury running and melding together until they formed a shining pool, a mirror in which to see herself.

The image Rachel saw was not her own but the triptych. On the central panel there were no angels to counterbalance the downward drag of the body lying in its mother's arms, no hint of dawn above the horizon to symbolize the resurrection. In refusing such pious conventions Adrianna Van Dyckhuizen had created a painting so stark, so beautiful, it was as if Christ's cry of abandonment from the cross had been taken up by the whole world, reverberating through human history until it was Rachel's turn to hear it. After the enormity of her violation, nothing could have spoken so authentically.

And yet the triptych was nothing like Mantegna's *Dead Christ*, a painting which exposed Christ to the viewer like a body in a morgue, utterly devoid of transcendence. Winged by side panels, the *Lamentation* formed the nucleus of a wider drama, a domestic and civic tragedy that not only commented on but validated the significance of what it witnessed. Stricken by the plague, the Van Dyckhuizen family and the city of Bruges could claim an intimate share in the suffering portrayed in the central panel, a correspondence extending into the present by the artist's fearless gaze. This was the grace the triptych bestowed, the significance of the *compassio* in the face of the Mother as she held her Son, that somehow, mysteriously, she was not a passive observer but a participant in the drama of salvation, a drama Adrianna not only shared but passed on, like a gift, to the viewer.

185

Suffering was not something to be borne alone, her gaze said, but could be shared, participated in, by another. It was this chain of correspondences, this link between one human being and another, between one age and the next, that Adrianna wished to convey. Without this connection, her painting implied, suffering would be an absurdity, a meaningless cruelty, the only response incomprehension and despair.

Chanting to its conclusion, the words of the Festival of Lights became stepping stones over the turbulence of Rachel's life, a place to rest before going on.

Brings mourners joy.

Framed by the doors, the central aisle stretched along the nave to converge on the altar and the motionless figure hanging on the cross above it. Rachel's eyes traveled up the smooth, wax-like torso, past the drooping head and on to the oriel of stained glass, its colors extinguished by night. Before the altar thronged the congregation. They held candles lit from the bonfire, each a pinpoint of light in that vast space, together a mighty radiance that illuminated the nave and dazzled Rachel's eyes.

A flame divided but undimmed.

Now Angelo was coming forward, a dumpy little figure bowing solemnly to the congregation before swinging the censer towards them for a blessing. As a body, the congregation returned his bow and Rachel found herself unexpectedly moved by this liturgical courtesy, this acknowledgment of a blessing bestowed.

Let it continue bravely burning to dispel the darkness of this night.

Earlier that evening Rachel had packed up her apartment. She stripped down the bed to the quilted diamonds of the bare mattress, stuffing the sheets and bedspread into a pillowcase which she left by the door for the landlady. Crossing the room, she stepped out onto the balcony.

The first night she spent in the apartment was cold and blustery with rain coming on. Even so she had felt the challenge of the triptych awaiting her, a promise ratified by the unexpected wave of a stranger from a window across the street.

The window was dark now although the shutters stood open to admit the mild spring air. The complicated odor of basil came to her from a nearby balcony garden. When Romans brought their house plants and herbs outside, began to eat *al fresco* at the street side cafes, it confirmed the arrival of spring. Soon tourists would be pouring off trains and buses, filling hotel rooms, milling in St. Peter's Square and the Forum, patiently lining up outside the Colosseum and the Pinacoteca, and Rome would put on its public face. Cafes and restaurants would stay open longer, sidewalk vendors would set up their carts under makeshift awnings, gypsy children would roam the streets with outstretched hands and musicians would play on street corners and at restaurant tables hoping for tips.

But beneath the bustle of a tourist city the quiet business of living would go on, steadily, imperceptibly, like the shuttle of a loom, weaving threads of connection between strangers and neighbors, between Rachel and the city that had graciously incorporated her into its design. She would chat with the woman at the market who sold her fruit, would ask about her husband and children; she would go with Angelo to a soccer match in the stadium and wave from across the square to the woman who came to Our Lady of Sorrows every week to arrange the flowers. Together she and Donati would walk in the Villa Borghese Gardens where the daffodils would be in full bell, where the tulips would even now be thrusting through the brown earth in their geometrical beds along the walkways, and they would watch for cygnets hatched under the greening canopy of the willows that grew on the island of the Temple of Aesculapius.

The morning after the press conference the papers had run the story of the Ferrara Museum's involvement with Apex, unleashing a torrent of indignant letters to the editor calling for an investigation and Persegati's resignation. Rachel phoned her mother to ask her to sub-let her Manhattan apartment on a six month, renewable lease. The enormous severance payment offered her when her curator in New York called to inform her that she was relieved of her position as senior medievalist, was clearly intended to encourage her to go quietly. She agreed. With the money she leased an apartment in Trastevere, depositing the rest in a bank in Rome, enough to live on for the foreseeable future.

Now that she had completed the task of unveiling, ensuring Adrianna would be known as one of the most accomplished painters and illuminators of her day, that the triptych would remain in the chapel of Our Lady of Sorrows, Rachel found herself oddly unconcerned about the future. Somehow the knowledge that the triptych would continue to offer those who saw it a tremor of consolation in the midst of a broken world, the same consolation Rachel herself had received, was enough.

"You sound happy," her mother said.

"I guess I am," Rachel replied.

"What will you do now?"

Monsignor Corolli at the Vatican Museums had called, offering to hire her and Donati as freelance conservators to restore work on site throughout Rome. Rachel told him she and Donati would get back to him after Easter.

"I'm not sure," Rachel replied. "Something will turn up."

Behind the altar, the monsignor cleaned the chalice with a white cloth, slipped the paten into its linen folder and placed it neatly on top of the cup. Suddenly stripped of the sacerdotal accouterments of gold and wine and bread, the altar became homely again, as functional, ordinary, as the table in Signora Donati's kitchen. Yet an echo of grandeur remained, the bare white cloth, the lit candles, a sign of readiness, a promise to the unexpected and weary guest of a welcome as unquestioning and generous as the one Rachel had been given when she put her lips to the spoon Signora Donati held out and tasted.

People were beginning to leave the church and Rachel and Donati withdrew into the shadows under the portico. Standing together, still mantled in the solemnity of the service, the church, the piazza, and further out in the darkness, the sprawling mystery of Rome itself, suddenly took on a vital clarity as if Rachel were witnessing a tableau of faith renewed, reaffirmed, reenacted again and again ad infinitum.

At last the church stood empty, the piazza cleared of parishioners chatting to one another, calling out a happy Easter. Even those who had come to see the triptych merely out of curiosity had drifted away in search of late night bars and cafes. Through the still open doors they could hear Angelo moving from pew to pew collecting hymnals and the voice of the monsignor asking him to lock up. Then the doors closed, one by one, and Rachel and Donati were alone, the only sound the faint whisper of the fountain in the middle of the square.